WHEN CUPID MISSED
A FEEL-GOOD ROMANTIC COMEDY

S J CRABB

♥

Copyrighted Material

Copyright © S J Crabb 2023

S J Crabb has asserted her rights under the Copyright, Designs and Patents Act 1988 to be identified as the Author of this work.

This book is a work of fiction and except in the case of historical fact, any resemblance to actual persons, living or dead, is purely coincidental.
All rights reserved. No part of this book may be reproduced or transmitted in any form without written permission of the author, except by a reviewer who may quote brief passages for review purposes only.

NB: This book uses UK spelling.

WHEN CUPID MISSED

This book was previously published as Will You by the same author.

Love looks not with the eyes, but with the mind, And therefore is winged Cupid painted blind. *William Shakespeare*

When a rival shop opens opposite, Nelly is shocked to discover it's owned by her schoolgirl crush. Jack Mason, captain of the football team and popular guy.

He was always well out of her league and being the nerdy daughter of the Headmaster, she never stood a chance.

Fast forward a few years and he's back in her life. However, love quickly turns to hate when your dream is threatened, and Nelly wastes no time in telling Jack exactly what she thinks of him.

However, Jack doesn't take the hint and has an indecent proposal for Nelly that she can't turn down.

When things get complicated, she wonders if she's made a huge mistake.

There's no backing out now, and it's not just Nelly and Jack who are struggling.

Cupid's arrows are missing every target and it will take a miracle to get happily ever after back on track.

For fans of feel-good romance. Enemies to lovers, fake relationships, small-town romance, unrequited love, and clean romance.

CHAPTER 1

The aroma hits me as soon as I open the door. It awakens my senses and calms my soul. Yes, this is what I love—an instant fix. Better than drugs and the only smell I ever want to savour — chocolate.

As I peer around the little shop, I smile to myself. I have a passion and it's all around me. Chocolate.

I knew what I wanted from a very early age and that was to open my own little shop selling the product that interests me the most. Luckily that dream came true and six months ago I opened the doors to my very own chocolate emporium. Chocolatti.

I never dread coming to work. In fact, I wish it came with a little flat above it, but unfortunately the one above this shop has a tenant already. Mr Bryan. He has lived here for close to twenty years and owns the freehold to the building. As landlords go, he's a good one and may be a little eccentric, but has a heart of gold. He pops down most days for a chat and I count my lucky stars that I found such a little piece of paradise so close to home.

Collingdale is a small town that just made the grade up

from a village. There aren't many shops but the ones here are interesting and different from the chains in the nearby larger town. It's a lovely place to be and a lot of the customers are regulars. I have grown quite fond of them and look forward to hearing about their everyday lives as they crowd through the doors every day.

Maybe crowd was the wrong word to use. More like a steady trickle – ok, a slow drip as they pop their heads around to say hi. Trade is ok but could be a lot better and I have to work doubly hard to meet the rent every month. However, I would open twenty-four hours a day if it meant making this business a success.

As I start the day, I shake off the worry at the door. It will be fine. Something will happen and everything will come good in the end. Maybe a busload of chocoholics will screech to a halt outside and spend their body weight in chocolate. Perhaps a Hollywood producer will decide this is the perfect location for his next blockbuster and pay me a year's takings to rent the shop for one week. Possibly an eccentric customer will donate a large proportion of their sudden lottery win to be kept in chocolate for a year and maybe fate will shine down on me and deliver me the customers I need every day just to keep this place going.

I hear the door chime and look up as Richie stumbles through the door.

"Nelly, darling, I need a fix of chocolate crunchies before I pass out."

Laughing, I reach for my friends' usual guilty pleasure and smile.

"I thought you were in Paris."

"I was. I came home last night a day earlier than planned because Roger's home today and I wanted to be here to welcome him home."

"How is he?"

Richie shrugs. "I don't know. I expect he'll fill us in on all the gory details later. You can see why I need the chocolate now."

I smile at him sympathetically. "Well, if you need any help, you know where I am."

He nods gratefully. "Thanks darling. I'll be taking you up on that offer before the day is out if I know my boyfriend."

Richie's boyfriend Roger has just had knee surgery. He's not the most ideal patient in the world and Richie will have his work cut out. Richie works as an Air Steward and is always off on some trip or another which will be difficult for Roger when he gets home.

He gazes across the street and says with interest, "Have you found out who your new neighbour is yet?"

I follow his stare and shrug. "No. The shop fitters have been there all week and told me the signs are going up today. Maybe that will give us a clue."

"Didn't you ask them what it's going to be?" He says with interest.

I shake my head. "I did, but they wouldn't say. They told me a guy has it and is turning it into some sort of coffee shop."

Richie appears excited. "That's great. Maybe they'll serve cake as well and then I can alternate between the two of you. Chocolate and cake, my two guilty pleasures."

I grin. "Are you sure about that? I'm guessing you have a few more vices up your sleeve than that."

He winks cheekily. "Chance would be a fine thing. Anyway, what about you? Have you decided that a life outside of this place would be something worth pursuing? I don't know, maybe in the form of a date or two?"

I reach out and grab the money he waves in my direction and shake my head sadly. "As you said, chance would be a fine thing. Where am I going to find my dream man in Collingdale? It's the only place I ever go and the average age is fifty."

The door chimes again and we look up as my friend Angela heads inside. "Guys, you'll never guess."

We peer at her expectantly as she lowers her voice, although I'm not sure who she thinks is listening. "I just saw movement in the window opposite. They're cleaning off the stuff covering the windows. I really hope it's a new dress shop. We could do with some Paris fashion in Collingdale."

Richie rolls his eyes. "As if Paris would come here. Most of the customers knit their own clothes or buy them from the charity shops. It's no wonder the high street's dying. This generation buy everything online and are so glued to their phones they wouldn't see a 'must have' outfit beckoning them in from a shop window unless it had .com after it."

We nod in agreement. It's true. The average age of my customers is fifty and so any shop opening needs to bear that in mind during their market research.

Angela squeals excitedly. "Look, a hand appeared at the window. They're cleaning that stuff off."

We peer out and I can see that she's right. A hand is systematically cleaning the swirly cleaning stuff that has obscured the windows and is revealing the shop behind the façade.

Just for a minute, we all look in silence, then Richie whispers, "It's definitely a man's hand."

Angela hisses. "It appears to have a strong arm on the end of it."

We crane our necks to get a better view and I try to make out what lies behind the person cleaning the windows. What on earth could they be selling?

The hole in the window gets bigger and we see the body attached to the arm causing Richie to say with excitement. "Hmm, he obviously works out. Look at that t-shirt straining to hold itself together. One false move and it will rip in two."

He moves closer to the window and I say in alarm, "Don't

let him see you watching him. Pretend to be choosing something from my display."

Richie makes a big show of fussing with the window display and Angela whispers, "Well? Can you see anything yet?"

"Only ever dream I've ever had involving a man, muscles and a naked torso."

Angela gasps and rushes over to join him, and I hear her sigh. "Wow, this must just be the best view I've ever had. What a body."

I can't help myself and make my way to the window to stare at this obvious demi god who is putting on a show.

As I reach the window, I gasp in horror, "What the hell?"

The silence says it all as I say angrily, "You have got to be kidding me."

My two friends share a look and Angela says timidly, "I'm sure it's not as bad as it looks."

Staring at them angrily, I shout, "Well, I'm not standing here waiting to find out. I'm going right over there and confront that man with the hands immediately."

An uncomfortable silence follows me as I stomp across the street with only one aim in mind. Stop this shop from ever opening and send this man with the hands and sexy body right back to where he came from.

CHAPTER 2

I'm not sure I see anything but the red mist before my eyes as I knock sharply on the window. A face peers out of the hole that's appeared and I gasp. I know him.

Just for a moment, we stare at one another and I'm not sure who is more shocked.

Jack Mason. I don't believe it. The guy from my class at school and the one I obsessed over for six long years. The captain of the football team and the subject of every school girl's fantasies.

He appears as shocked as me and then I remember why I'm here and point to the sign that's just revealed itself and frown.

He looks confused, and then the penny drops as I tap my foot angrily on the pavement outside. Grinning sheepishly, he shrugs and moves away from the window, and I wait for him to open the door. Meanwhile, the sign mocks me with its devastating words.

'More Than Chocolate.'

If this is what I think it is, I have just seen my happy ever after being threatened cruelly. More than chocolate indeed. If there is one hint of the dark stuff in there, I will lose any cool I have tried to master. Nobody is opening across the street in direct competition with me if I have anything to do with it.

The door opens and I try not to let the sight of that torso sway me from my anger. Apparently, cleaning windows is hot work because Jack flaming Mason has stripped to the waist and his abs are doing some sort of strange workout before my very eyes.

Punching the giggling girl from school firmly back to the past where she belongs, I place my hands on my hips and glare at him angrily, saying tightly, "Do you care to explain yourself?"

He looks amused, which instantly makes me want to punch him in that tempting mouth.

"Well, well, Nelly Gray. Fancy seeing you here."

Trying to keep the surprise from my voice that he even remembers me, I say tartly, "Enough with the pleasantries. What the hell is going on? This had better not be what I think it is."

He grins. "What do you think it is?"

Rolling my eyes, I say slowly, as if talking to an idiot, "Well, 'more than chocolate' may indicate the presence of actual chocolate within these premises. As you can see, I have a chocolate shop in town and so there is no room for any more. Maybe you should just change direction before you make a fool of yourself. I mean, what were you thinking, opening in direct competition to an established business? Collingdale isn't big enough for two chocolate shops, especially opposite one another. What sort of business course did you attend if you thought that was a good idea?"

Jack shrugs. "What's the matter Nelly? Are you afraid the good people of this town will prefer my shop to yours?"

I almost can't speak with anger. "Are you serious? I mean, did one of those footballs from school hit you on the head and knock all the sense out of you? There is absolutely no way on earth I'm going to stand for this, do you hear me? Change direction immediately or get out of town. You have been warned."

To my intense irritation, he starts to laugh. Placing my hands on my hips, I glare at him and if looks could kill, he would be experiencing a slow, painful death by now.

He moves closer and I swallow hard.

Suddenly, it all comes flooding back. The childhood crush on the coolest guy in school. The endless dreams as I stole a look from across the room as he flexed his muscles at the back of the class. The jealousy, as I watched him openly flirt with every passable girl for miles, except me it seemed, and the anguish when he started dated princess popular who I hated with a passion. Now he's staring at me with that look, and I absolutely hate myself for instantly forgiving him on the spot. Why am I now hoping he sees me as something a bit more than Nelly Gray? The slightly odd girl, who shrank in her seat at the front of the class and was left out of every friendship group in the building because her father was the flaming headmaster?

He leans forward and time stands still. I watch with fascination as his eyes hold mine and twinkle with the confidence of a man who knows he can have anything he wants in life. I almost forget to breathe as he speaks in the lazy voice that used to make my heart flutter.

"As the name suggests, darling, it's more than chocolate. Lots more, to be precise. The chocolate probably makes up one per cent of my stock because this emporium is my coffee shop/gift shop. If the locals want chocolate, they won't find anywhere near as many varieties in here as they will across the road. Happy?"

I am actually speechless. Am I happy? Absolutely not if you think having a rival shop open its doors opposite, run by the local love god is good business sense. However, the girl I was is deliriously happy that he is moving in. Eye candy of the sweetest kind. The man whose name adorned my school books with a heart surrounding it. My name coupled with his as I imagined the impossible and dreamt we were a couple. This is the stuff of dreams and nightmares combined and for once, I am shocked into silence.

So, I do what I've always done when faced with a situation out of my comfort zone. I turn and walk away.

As I head back to Chocolatti, my heart thumps with every step I take. Jack Mason is here! In my sights and working opposite me every day. Surely a ruined business is a small price to pay for such a treat. I expect I'm overreacting. I mean, he's so popular he will certainly draw the crowds. Yes, this is working out very well, actually. Maybe this is a gift from God; God's gift himself. Yes, what a great idea. A rival made from my dreams who has come to enrich my life.

Then reality bites.

This is a disaster.

I'll be out of business within a month. Who will want to come to my shop when he's across the road? The tears well behind my eyes and I feel so out of control it hurts. I can't compete with him. This is the end of life as I know it.

Trying to put on a brave face, I head back inside my shop and Richie says hesitatingly, "What did you say?"

Shrugging, I put on my brave face and say nonchalantly, "He thinks he can open up in direct competition with me, but I set him straight. I told him, using some very forceful words I might add, that I am most unhappy about the situation. I warned him what would happen if he dares open those doors to the paying public. In fact, I'm quite pleased with how I dealt with that situation. Yes, you should have heard me. I was magnificent."

Angela stares at me through wide eyes. "But that's Jack Mason. The Jack Mason. You know, the boy you used to…"

"Yes, well, enough about all that schoolgirl stupidity. It might have escaped your notice, Angela, but I have somewhat matured since my schooldays and men like Jack don't figure in my plans at all. In fact, when I just saw him close up, I wondered what I ever saw in him. Good grief, what was I thinking, all brawn and no brain? Definitely not my type at all."

"So, what is your type?"

I freeze on the spot and my friend's expressions confirm my worst fears.

He's here.

CHAPTER 3

*A*s I spin around, I see him lounging casually on the door frame as he stares at me with amusement.

I try to act as if nothing happened and say haughtily, "I'm sorry, may I help you with a purchase?"

He laughs, which instantly gets my back up and saunters into my shop like any other paying customer. Grabbing a few packets of chocolate off the shelf, he places them on the counter and grins.

"I'll have these please and while you're packing them up, you can answer my question. What is your type?"

I grab the chocolate and, shrugging, place them in a bag. "That will be ten pounds please and as for my type, well, somebody intellectual, definitely not into sports. A man who speaks many languages, preferably with a French accent. Somebody well-travelled and successful with his own company and a staff of hundreds. A helicopter would be nice, oh, and a house in the country as well as one in the town. Somebody who loves the theatre and the arts who thinks learning Chinese and volunteering in third world countries is a great holiday experience. Yes, definitely not someone shallow, obviously vain and obsessed with his looks with a passion for airheads. Oh no, definitely not that sort of guy who has so few brain cells he thinks opening a shop in direct competition with another business in a small town is good business practice. Anyway, if that's all, have a nice day and goodbye."

There's an awkward silence and I can tell Richie and Angela are trying hard not to laugh. However, Jack just nods and smiles. "Well, thanks for the chocolate. Maybe I can return the favour sometime. You should come to my opening evening. Only close friends and family are invited. You can all count yourself on that list."

I'm appalled when Richie and Angela nod their heads vigorously and say with excitement, "Wow, thanks. You can count on us being there."

I just glare at him and try to keep my eyes above his neck because he appears to have forgotten that it's bad manners to walk around without a shirt on.

I say tightly, "I'm sorry. I have plans that night."

He laughs, "I haven't told you when it is."

My so-called friends snigger and, after throwing them the death stare, I say in a bored voice. "Any evenings are out because I have a very busy schedule. Between the various martial arts lessons I take and the many dates I have arranged, I just don't have the time. Anyway, why would I support you when you have shown no regard for my business? No, there will be no friendly banter between us and no cosy little get togethers. If you sell one chunk of chocolate in that shop opposite, we are officially at war."

He shakes his head and smiles, which makes me forget just for a minute why I should hate him.

"I'm sorry you feel that way. Maybe when you get over the initial shock, you'll change your mind."

He turns to my friends and smiles. "Tuesday evening, seven thirty. I hope to see you both there."

As he heads outside, I try not to stare at his retreating figure and sigh like a fangirl.

Instead, I turn my anger on the two traitors in my midst and say shortly, "Thanks for the solidarity, guys. I can't believe you're really going to his stupid party."

Richie shrugs. "Of course. I'm going to check out the competition on your behalf. Haven't you heard of the enemy within? I will suss out the competition and report back. It's genius if you ask me."

Angela nods frantically. "Same for me. You know, this could work to our advantage. We will be your eyes and ears and then we can put the word out that it's not worth going there. Don't worry, Nelly, you can count on us. Leave it with us. We have your back."

She then makes a big show of gazing at her watch. "Goodness, is that the time? I must run. Later babes."

Richie seizes his chance and says brightly, "I'm right behind you. Roger will be back soon, and I haven't ironed the flannels yet. See you later, Nelly."

As the door closes firmly behind them, I sigh heavily. Great. This could just be my worst day ever.

Typically, this is a quiet day. In fact, most days are and so I busy myself with tidying the shop while trying not to attack the stock with a deep depression. I always do this when I'm down. My love of chocolate extends to it being the cure for everything in my life. The endless dates that lead nowhere. The fact I'm struggling to make ends meet and have nothing to occupy me outside of my working hours. I totally lied when I told Jack I didn't have time for his so-called party. I have more time than anyone I know and now I'm in an even worse mood than before. To make matters worse, the only customer I have in the next hour comes in to complain about the chocolate melting on their way home. I tried to explain that you shouldn't leave it in a hot car while you go and do your grocery shopping, but she was having none of it.

So, by the time the desired lunchtime rush is over, I resort to the usual pick me up and cram as many chocolate balls into my mouth as I can. This is a habit I really should try to break because almost immediately, the door opens and Mrs Mulligan comes in, saying quickly, "Afternoon, Nelly. I need an order of chocolate Brazils as quickly as possible because I'm double parked."

As I turn to face her, I watch her expression change to one of surprise as she sees my cheeks bulging with chocolate. Shaking her head, she says imperiously, "Eating the stock again, my dear? Maybe a chocolate shop isn't really the best thing for you. I mean, you should watch your weight at your age, not to mention it's bad for your teeth. After all, eating the profits won't please the bank manager and I should know, I'm married to him."

I try hard to swallow some of the chocolate but I rammed so much in there's no room for manoeuvre. Instead, I just grab a little box from the shelf and start weighing out the chocolates, while trying to have a conversation with just expressions alone.

To say this is awkward is an understatement, and I feel mortified at the pitying glances she throws at me. By the time she leaves, I never uttered one word and had to point to the digital display on the cash register to tell her how much it was. In fact, it takes a good five minutes for the chocolate to melt and as it slides down my throat, I feel sick. Not from the chocolate, but from the fact I allowed myself to weaken.

The downside to running a chocolate shop is the temptation involved. Unless I'm busy, I start to eye up the stock like a cannibal stalking its human prey. Those little delicious squares of heaven call to the weaker part of me that can't say no. They settle on my hips and surround my stomach and leave me feeling like an addict coming down from a high. I loathe myself and vow to never do it again until the next little temptation rears its pretty little head and shouts to me how delicious it is. I've even taken to jogging and doing stretching exercises when the customers aren't around, just to shift any calories that are piling on quicker than I can burn them off.

So, unfortunately, it's when I'm doing squats that I'm aware I'm not alone.

Spinning around, my face turns redder than the delicious red velvet chocolates I have in the chiller cabinet, when I see Jack smirking at me over the counter.

So, to disguise my embarrassment, I go on the attack. "What do you want? You had better be coming to tell me you've agreed to my demands."

He smiles sweetly and my body reacts accordingly, which makes me hate it even more than I did before.

He peers at me with amusement and points to my face, saying, "I think you may have forgotten the bit on your lower lip."

Running my tongue around my lips, the delicious taste of chocolate balls reveals itself and I feel my cheeks flame with embarrassment as I glare at him.

He says softly, "Listen, I think we got off on the wrong foot earlier. I want to start again, if that's possible."

I shrug. "Only if you ditch the chocolate."

He says firmly. "I told you there really isn't much of it involved. Anyway, I can't because I've had all the signs printed, the chocolate ordered, and the company registered. It's too late."

I don't know why, but I start jogging on the spot and say breathlessly, "Then you can leave. In case it's escaped your attention, this is my exercise period. You are interrupting a very important part of my day with your idle chatter and I need you to leave - immediately."

He throws me an odd look, which is probably due to the fact I am now doing star jumps, but it does the trick and he starts heading towards the door. As he makes to leave, he says loudly, "Please come on Tuesday. I'm sure we can work this out."

I turn my back on him and hear the door click shut, leaving me feeling like a total bitch. Way to go Nelly. Make an enemy of the one boy you have ever loved who never once acknowledged your existence. Now he is you are making yourself look like a complete and utter bitch.

Reaching for the chocolate covered nuts, I reason with myself that they are only half bad for me as I systematically work my way through the packet and berate myself for every weak part of me that just can't ever seem to get it right.

CHAPTER 4

For the next few days, I avoid Jack Mason. I watch through a mirror I've set up in the corner to monitor the progress opposite and despite everything the shop looks amazing. Tables and chairs now sit on the once empty pavement. Striped canopies entice people inside and the window is dressed in tempting gifts and the promise of a calming latte while the customers consider beautiful things they instantly need. Even I admit it's impressive and, as he said, nothing like my shop at all. Maybe he is only selling a few bars of chocolate, but that's still too many in my book.

Tuesday comes and as I shut up my little shop, I think about the evening ahead. Maybe I should go and offer the olive branch of friendship. We are both in business and should support one another and, who knows, we may become friends and associates. We could join the chamber of commerce together and share lifts to the meetings. Swap business tips and ideas and make Collingdale a better place to visit based on our suggestions at the local council meetings.

Maybe we would discover a shared love of all things chocolate and laugh at these first few days and just maybe, Jack and I could become friends… with benefits. Yes, I'm liking that idea. Benefits of the most delicious kind. Wild nights of passion involving lots of melted chocolate and no inhibitions. He will confess that he always desired me from afar but found me too intimidating due to my utter perfection to pluck up the courage to talk to me. Yes, that's what will happen.

I'm guessing I should drag on something sexy and visit his little party and show him that I'm the bigger person in all this. Yes, that's what I'll do for the sake of my business, and so with a newfound resolve, I head home to change.

* * *

As I outside More Than Chocolate, I am already having second thoughts. I can tell his party has started because the noise is deafening. There are hordes of people inside, and I feel a little intimidated. Perhaps I should just slide off and leave them to it. I almost do, but then see Richie and Angela advancing towards me with excitement written all over their faces.

Richie shouts, "Nelly, darling, I'm so glad you came. Come in with us and we can suss everything out together."

I nod gratefully, thinking this is the best option. Show my face with my friends and then make my polite excuses to leave.

Feeling a little braver, I set myself between them and we head inside.

As shops go, this one's impressive. Even I can see no expense has been spared and the professional shop fitting company he used has done him proud. All around is temptation in every form. Beautiful gifts nestle on stylishly arranged tables. Calming music plays from the speakers and the smell of coffee and baking bread mingles with the perfumes of the scented candles and reed diffusers. Little white tables and chairs hold pretty flowers in jam jars and then I see the biggest temptation on offer in this establishment, Jack Mason himself.

Our eyes connect across the shop and he smiles happily. I can't seem to look away but try my best to look indifferent as he moves across and says warmly, "It's good of you to come; let me show you around."

I shake my head and, stepping back, say, "Oh, it's fine. You should see to your guests. We'll find our own way around."

He says firmly, "Nonsense. I want to look after you personally."

My legs shake along with my heart as he takes my arm and guides me through the crowd, saying with obvious pride, "Really, I'm so glad you came. I want to show you that you have absolutely nothing to worry about."

The trouble is, I have everything to worry about because suddenly I am that girl again. Smelly Nelly, the headmaster's daughter and enemy of every child in the school. The girl with braces, pigtails and sensible shoes who wore strictly regulation uniform with not a hair out of place. That straight-A student who served on every committee possible. The student president and organiser of every boring event going, who was made to attend each function at the school as the hired help because that was expected. Even the teachers treated me differently for fear of drawing my father's attention and tonight I am reminded of every excruciating minute of it because sitting holding court in the centre of the room is princess popular herself, Emma Grant.

I feel the life drain from me as she glances up and sees me standing before her with Jack's hand on my arm. Her eyes narrow and she appears confused. She doesn't look as if she remembers me because I am now completely different. I dyed my hair years ago. The endless gym sessions after work have shifted most of the pounds, and the braces vacated my mouth years ago. I have grown taller and dress as fashionably as my meagre wages will allow. In fact, I am officially a different person until Jack says loudly, "You remember Nelly Gray, the headmaster's daughter, don't you guys?"

All eyes swivel in my direction, and there they are. The popular gang. Alive and well and staring at me with derision, as they always did.

Princess Emma tosses back her long, black hair and looks me up and down, saying disdainfully, "Goodness, I would never have remembered you. You look totally different."

Her friend Madison nods. "Yes, didn't we used to call you Smelly Nelly?"

They all snigger and my face flames with embarrassment. It doesn't matter how I look now; how successful I am, or the fact I'm standing with their leader's hand on my arm, I will always be that social pariah, and nothing will ever change.

However, I am not that girl anymore so, I draw myself up and smile at Emma coolly. "Yes, I remember you, Emma. Good to see you again. I think the last time I did was when your parents were called in after you were found snogging that French exchange student in the boy's changing rooms. What was his name? Oh yes, Pierre, how original. Never mind, I'm sure it helped with your French… um… kissing skills. After all, if I remember correctly, you didn't have many other ones to fall back on. Oh, and Madison, I remember you. You were the girl everyone voted most likely to have a kid first. Did you ever manage it? It would be such fun if you did. Goodness, how cruel kids can be. I should know because every single one of you made my life hell back then. I wish I could say it didn't matter, but actually, it did. You see, every hateful word you said, every spiteful look you gave me, and every time you made me feel like dirt on your shoe mattered. You were bullies of the worst kind and it's only now I thank God I was never actually accepted as one of you because who would want to be classed as shallow, vindictive, ugly bullies, who never amounted to anything? Well, it's been good to catch up, but the air is somewhat stale in here so, I'll leave you to your shallow lives and carry on with being much better than you."

Turning away, I almost run to the door and as the cooler air hits me, I gasp for oxygen. Then, a firm hand grabs me and pulls me back against that infernally hard chest and strong arms wrap around me as Jack growls, "Not so fast. You're going nowhere. You're my guest and if anyone's leaving, it's them."

I peer up at him in surprise, and he smiles gently. "I'm sorry about that, Nelly. Every word you just said is true. We made your life hell at school and nobody regrets that more than me. I recognised you as soon as I saw your angry face peering through that window, and now I want to make it up to you."

I stare at him in surprise. "What do you mean, make it up to me?"

For some reason, the world stops spinning. Something about the look in his eyes tells me everything is about to change. This is a moment in time that alters the future and shifts destinies.

I'm aware we have quite an audience as the music stops playing and the crowds inside stop to stare.

Then Jack kneels before me, takes my hand in his and says in a loud voice. "Will you be my girlfriend, Nelly Gray?"

Just for a second, I think I'd heard him incorrectly. "I'm sorry. What did you say?"

He smiles a little self-consciously and says softly, "I said, will you be my girlfriend?"

Shaking my head, I look at his slightly anxious face and then at the faces all around me. Richie and Angela are staring at us in disbelief and the popular gang appear as shocked as I am.

Then I see the smirk on Emma's face and the anger returns, making me hiss. "Is this how you get your kicks? Making a fool out of me again in front of your friends. Well, go to Hell. Pick on someone who wants your attention and leave me alone."

I turn away and find a new skill in running. Actually, I sprint like an Olympic athlete away from the crowd, who start laughing. The tears blind my view as Emma's shrill voice calls out, "Nice one, Jack. You had us there for a moment."

I feel like such a fool and curse my bad judgement in coming here in the first place. As I reach my car, I struggle with the keys and shakily try to get them in the lock. They fall to the floor and I curse as I drop to my knees and search for them where they rolled under the car. Then I'm aware that someone is running closer and steel myself for more public humiliation.

Jack drops to his knees beside me and says earnestly, "Please listen to me, Nelly. I promise you that wasn't some cruel stunt. I really meant it."

Noting we're alone, I stare at him with a pained expression and say in a whisper, "Why?"

He sighs heavily. "I have my reasons, but now isn't the time to tell you. Meet me tomorrow after work and I'll explain everything, that is, if you haven't already got a prior engagement?"

He smiles sweetly and I notice it appears a genuine one, so I nod. "Ok, I'll hear you out. Though I can't think why you did that. It's very odd."

He holds out my keys and smiles. "Odd doesn't begin to describe my life at the moment. However, I can assure you I'm not some mad weirdo who gets his kicks from messing with women's minds. I have a very valid reason for everything and think it will work to your advantage."

As I take the keys from his hand, my fingers brush against his and a shiver passes through me. Yes, Jack Mason has always had that effect on me. The sort that makes rational thought impossible. When he said those words to me tonight, it was a re-run of every fantasy I ever had about him. Dating Jack at school would have shown everyone. All those girls who made my life hell would be forced to admit I had won. What Jack did tonight was what I've always wanted – wasn't it? Then why do I get the feeling there is more to this than meets the eye? There is something going on in his life that he's hiding and tomorrow I may discover what that is.

As I stand, I look him in the eye and say with practised disinterest, "OK, you can have your say tomorrow but I'm warning you, if I don't like what I hear, we are officially enemies."

He nods, looking slightly guilty. "I'll look forward to it and thanks for giving me the chance."

I don't say another word and just get in the car and leave him standing on the side of the road as I drive home.

Well, if anything, tomorrow will be interesting.

CHAPTER 5

The next day drags interminably. The clock couldn't go any slower and I find myself glancing in the spy mirror I've set up many times throughout the day. The only distraction is when Ken drops in for a chat.

As the door chimes, I look up and stifle a smile as I see him filling the doorway wearing a Hawaiian shirt, holding a tray of six eggs.

"Morning Nelly. I brought you some eggs from Patty's farm."

Patty is his long-suffering girlfriend. I say girl, more a woman and they have been dating for twenty years. He insists on them living in different houses because he says the farm she owns stinks to high heaven and the cows annoy him with their constant mooing. She won't leave her babies, as she calls the cows, for living in the town and turning her back on nature. As a result, they meet up twice a week at her house and twice at his. The rest of the time, they either go to friends or indulge in their hobbies. Ken is currently into pottery and made me a wonky jug for my birthday.

Smiling, I beckon him inside. "Hey, Ken, how is the gorgeous Patty?"

He shrugs. "Last I saw of her, she had her hand up a cow's backside. Hardly the stuff of erotic fantasies."

Laughing, I offer him his favourite chocolate from the chiller cabinet.

He nods over to More Than Chocolate. "What's going on there?"

I stare at him gloomily. "A rival has moved into town and I'm not sure what to do about it."

He raises his eyes. "Do you want me to threaten him?"

"With what? You're hardly the godfather, Ken."

He winks. "How do you know? Anyway, I would just be protecting my investment."

"It's fine. We're meeting up later to discuss things. Hopefully, it won't be so bad."

He sits on the floor cross-legged and rather than think it strange; I take a moment to marvel at his flexibility before joining him.

We stare across the road and Ken sighs. "Why is life so difficult?"

I glance at him in surprise. "What's so difficult about your life?"

He shakes his head and appears a little sad. "Patty's sister's husbands just left her. Fifty years of marriage down the drain. Apparently, she came home one day and found him in bed with their neighbour, Madge Arnold. It wasn't the first time by all accounts, and now he's moved in with Madge."

I stare at him in horror. "That's terrible, poor Sandra."

He nods gloomily. "Poor Patty you mean. Sandra wants to come and stay and knowing her, she'll never leave. She's always been difficult, and Patty can't stand her. The trouble is, blood counts for a lot and she can't say no. Patty can't leave her on her own to come and stay with me, so it looks like I'll be spending more time there. It's an impossible situation."

I smile sympathetically. "At least you have someone. I don't. Maybe in life, some of us never find that special someone. Maybe love passes us by and we must watch others enjoying what will never be ours and just congratulate ourselves on a tidy home and a selfish life. It's good to be able to call the shots and not consider anyone's feelings. I don't have to wash anyone else's clothes or listen to their boring chatter when all I want to do is watch reality TV. My bed is my own and the toilet seat is always neatly down. My life is orderly and just how I want it but it's still missing a vital ingredient that makes life worth living. Someone to share it with. If I were in your shoes, I'd be grateful for every minute you spend with Patty because, as Sandra is about to find out, it's lonely living on your own and loneliness is too high a price to pay for a selfish life."

Reaching out, Ken squeezes my hand and says softly, "You're young and won't be lonely for long. You have youth on your side and think you'll live forever. One day, everything will make sense and it's up to you to seize that moment when it comes. Maybe Patty and I should have married all those years ago. Maybe we still will. Will it make a difference in our lives? Probably not for the better. Just remember to throw caution to the wind sometimes and take a chance on madness. There is no rule book when it comes to relationships other than to cherish them when you find the real deal. Whatever happens with Patty, I will always value that above everything."

Smiling, I glance across the road. "Well, life is certainly strange at the moment. I'll keep you posted on developments when they occur."

He gazes around the shop and says sadly, "How's trade?"

Shrugging, I smile bravely. "It's getting there. We had a good Valentine's Day and Easter is around the corner. I could do without the competition, but if anything, it may make me pull my socks up and think of a few ways to attract extra business in. This could be the making of Chocolatti, and after all, a bit of healthy competition never hurt anyone."

Ken stands and pulls me up. "Do you fancy a cuppa?"

I nod. "I thought you'd never ask."

He heads upstairs to make me the desired cup of tea and I think about what he said. Maybe I should listen to what Jack has to say and not react immediately. Who knows, it may even add a little excitement to my life.

CHAPTER 6

By the time I finish cashing up on another underwhelming day, Jack is waiting for me outside. Seeing him standing there takes me back to those damn fantasies again, where he was my boyfriend, and I was the envy of every girl in school. Funny how life works out. I never thought in a million years I would ever see him again, let alone be going on a... whatever this is.

He glances up and smiles, and my heart flutters. He always was impressive, and the years have been good to him. He has matured like a vintage piece of exotic cheese, a fine wine and a valuable piece of art. Smiling to myself at the thought, I'm surprised when he laughs and raises his eyes. "What's so funny?"

I shrug. "I was just thinking you look a little... um... cheesy standing there."

I giggle at his surprised expression, and he smiles sweetly. "You know, Nelly, you surprise me every day. When I saw you again, that was the first surprise. You've changed a lot since school."

I say with curiosity. "In what way?"

"I don't know. You have a confidence that wasn't there before. You really showed it to me when you felt challenged and, well, I kind of like the new you."

Shrugging, I try not to let him see how happy his words make me. "So what, people change? They grow up and mature. You know, like a fine cheese."

I giggle again at his confused expression and then he laughs, making me stop and listen to that laugh because it changes everything. Jack Mason has never looked more desirable than at this moment. Gone is the cocky, self-assured football demigod from school. In his place is a guy at ease with himself. He appears comfortable with who he is. Maybe that's the result of always getting everything you want in life – a certain confidence that infects those around you.

His eyes soften and he says gently, "I'm sorry."

"For what?"

"For not seeing you before."

My expression must be completely baffled because he gazes at me apologetically.

"I never saw you as a person at school. You were just that girl in class. The one who sat at the front and the perfect student. I didn't give you a second glance because there was nothing I wanted to look at. I was blinded by the obvious and never saw the amazing. I just want you to know that, Nelly, because I'm guessing it's something you haven't heard before."

I stare at him in complete shock and then glance around in case he's talking to somebody else. He has completely stolen every rational thought and smart word I have and stripped away every ounce of fight left in me with just a few words. Man, he's good. I must credit him that at least.

I drag myself back to reality and say firmly, "Well, enough of the small talk. What's happening here?"

He grins and nods towards a sports car parked nearby. "I'd like to take you to dinner and discuss our future."

We start to walk, and I say icily, "We don't have a future all the time you insist on selling chocolate in your fancy new shop."

He opens the passenger door like a true gentleman and says in a whisper that melts every inch of resolve in me, "I hope that by the end of the evening, you will see things differently. We do have a future, Nelly, and you are the one holding it in your hands like a delicate flower. If you crush it and throw it aside, the beauty will be gone forever. Nurture it and allow it to flourish and you will see how breath-taking it can be."

He winks as he closes the door firmly, leaving me wondering if he's had one too many bumps on the head on that football field. Who talks like that these days? Certainly not the popular, cool boy from the football team deeply rooted in my past. He's up to something and I need to keep my wits about me because I may be desperate for any little shred of male attention, but I'm no fool and I won't be treated like one.

The drive to wherever we're going is a silent one. If you don't count the soft rock ballads he plays in the car. Songs of eternal love and finding your soul mate were probably selected to get me in the mood to agree to whatever he wants. I'm not stupid. This man wants something from me, and I'm not prepared to play the gullible fool who will make it easy for him.

* * *

We pull up outside a fine restaurant in the larger town nearby. I could never afford to eat here, certainly not on the meagre wages I pay myself, and I feel a little uncomfortable. What if he wants to share the cost? My card would bounce quicker than the ball that obviously bounced off his head, and my mortification would be complete.

As if sensing my predicament, he says brightly, "I hope

you're hungry. This is my treat tonight; I insist before you start protesting and expecting to pay your own way."

I shrug, disguising the relief and say airily, "If you insist, although I expect you to get the receipt and offset it against expenses. That's the only way I'll agree if it's classed as a business meeting."

He grins. "Of course. A business meeting. If that's how you want to play it that's fine by me."

Feeling a little more confident now I can face this as a business meeting, I follow him inside the posh restaurant.

All around us is pure wealth. Classical music plays and the décor shrieks opulence with pristine white tablecloths covering small tables, holding silver cutlery and crystal cut glasses. Mirrors line the walls and various ornamental plants hug corners, creating privacy for those tables that require a more discreet dining experience. As it's early, there aren't many occupied tables and I'm surprised when the waiter directs us to one of the intimate tables hidden from public view.

Jack smiles as the waiter pulls the chair out for me and takes his seat opposite. I am so out of my comfort zone here and he knows it. What's he playing at?

Jack orders us a bottle of wine and I'm glad of it. I wouldn't know what to ask for because I'm just usually guided by price and choose the cheapest one on offer. This would be no exception, so for once, I'm happy to leave it to him. After all, this is his party, and he's footing the bill.

Then we're alone and he stares at me with a hint of uncertainty in his eyes that makes me more confused than ever. Whatever this is, he's worried. He wants something and I'm not stupid enough to think that he has fallen completely in love with me after just one look. This must be about my business. Maybe he wants me to close and pave the way for his own success. Perhaps he's here to lay on the charm, so I agree to every demand he throws me to guarantee his future.

The waiter returns and fills our glasses, which I'm grateful for. I think a good, deep, glug of alcohol is needed because I may not like what I'm about to hear.

I feel so jittery I almost can't see the menu and it's not because I forgot my reading glasses. In the end, I opt for the only thing I can see: salmon en-croute.

Jack smiles and says charmingly, "That sounds delicious. Make that two."

Briefly, I wonder if he needs glasses too. Feeling a little amused at the thought, I take another slug of wine and face him with my new friend confidence sitting right beside me in the wine glass.

"Well, Jack, this is very nice and all, but I think you have some explaining to do, don't you?"

He has the grace to look a little embarrassed and says in a low voice. "Yes, I believe I owe you an explanation. I'm sorry about my outburst yesterday, but I want you to know I meant every word. I do want you to be my girlfriend."

I almost spit my wine across the table as I say weakly, "But why?"

He shakes his head. "Please don't hate me for what I'm about to say, but you are possibly the only girl I know who can help me here."

He smiles apologetically. "You see, my life has just spiralled into a crazy vortex that I never saw coming. I have an old aunt Alice, who is, shall we say, quite a character. Well, she's made this will, you know, a sort of living will and wants to see it carried out to the letter."

I say sympathetically, "The poor woman. I'm so sorry, Jack. Does it involve some sort of euthanasia or a visit to Dignitas because I'm sorry if you're asking me to put your aunt out of her misery, all the fine dining in the world won't make me agree to that?"

WHEN CUPID MISSED

Jack starts laughing and I stare at him in shock. "What's so funny? Death is nothing to laugh about, you know?"

He shakes his head and grins. "She's not dying, Nelly. Well, at least I don't think she is. In fact, she will probably outlive us all."

The confusion must show on my face because he says gently. "I'll explain, but it's a little strange. Aunt Alice has made this living will, which means if we, that is the family, carry out her wishes, she will transfer our inheritance to us while she's still alive. She told us her one wish was to see us using her money and getting the benefit of it, but we had to prove we were worthy of it first."

I gaze at him in complete confusion. "I'm sorry, I don't understand. What has any of that got to do with me?"

He regards me with a strange look and seems quite vulnerable and a little worried as he says tentatively, "She has set each member of the family individual tasks they must accomplish by the end of the year. If we can prove to her we have carried her wishes out to the letter, she will transfer our share of the inheritance."

Despite the strangeness of the conversation, I am riveted. "Wow, this sounds like something out of a movie. What do you have to do?"

He appears slightly embarrassed. "Well, Aunt Alice is growing tired of my playboy lifestyle, as she calls it. She, in no uncertain terms, told me to grow up and take responsibility for my life. I had to open a business from scratch and make it work. If I could show that I had put everything into it to make it a success, she would honour her end of the deal."

I frown and say coolly, "I thought as much. You're here to decimate the competition. Pave the way for your own success by forcing the closure of the only other shop in town. Now I know why you opened opposite me. It was always your plan to drive me out but uh no buddy, you chose to mess with the wrong girl."

To his credit, Jack looks surprised and shakes his head vigorously. "No, I promise that isn't the reason. The shop was never my choice, anyway. Do you really think if I had a choice, I would open a girly gift shop and coffee shop? No, if I had my way, I would have opened a sports shop or a bicycle one. Something a lot more manly than More Than Chocolate."

I huff with exasperation. "Oh, for goodness' sake, Jack, you're talking in riddles. I'm no further forward to finding out why you want me to be your girlfriend. Is it so you can charm me into closing my shop in favour of yours? If so, it's a ridiculous idea and will fail immediately."

He seems shocked. "Is that's what you think? That I want to drive you out of business?"

I shrug and spin the wine glass around in my hands as I try to appear unconcerned in my guise as a hard-nosed businesswoman. Difficult when just the sight of those panty melting eyes is doing things to me that I only wrote about in my secret diary. Then I'm uncomfortable when I try to remember where that is. Goodness, if Jack, or anyone else come to mention it, ever found that ticking time bomb, I would close my shop as fast as possible and emigrate to Australia, actually no, New Zealand and live in the wild bush where nobody could taunt me with it.

Jack shakes his head and says softly, "The business is only one part of my task. The reason I chose More Than Chocolate was because it was always Aunt Alice's dream. She often spoke about the one regret in her life which was not opening her own little shop selling beautiful gifts. The coffee part was my idea because, as we all know, these days people always have time and money to spend on a coffee. I just thought it made good business sense."

Admonishing myself for not thinking of it first, I shrug and say in a cold voice, "The chocolate. What's the story there?"

He smiles guiltily. "I never thought about it, if I'm honest. I just decided on the name and then thought I should offer some chocolate. It was never about putting you out of business, or even competing with you in any way."

Part of me wants to believe him, but I still can't let it go. "So, why opposite me then? You must have known I'd be upset."

I'm shocked when he reaches across the table and takes my hand, squeezing it reassuringly. I know I should pull away, but it feels kind of nice being there and instead, I look at my hand in his and just note how small mine is in comparison. Jack's hand is tanned and capable and feels strong and comforting.

Pushing away the thought of what else he could do with his hands, I pull away as if I've been shocked and snarl, "Stop beating around the bush, Jack and tell me straight. Why did you ask me to be your girlfriend?"

He laughs nervously. "That was the other part of the deal. Aunt Alice is fed up with my playboy lifestyle and wants me to change my ways before she will part with one penny in my direction."

He shrugs and peers at me hopefully making me say wearily, "So, why me, Jack? I'm pretty sure you have your pick of women eager to fulfil the terms of the will. Prettier girls, you know, the sort you're used to. Why would you choose a girl you never gave the time of day and didn't even speak to before? It doesn't make sense."

He has the grace to look embarrassed and says warily, "Because I am everything my aunt thinks I am. I'm not ready to commit to one girl. Maybe I never will be. If I asked one of those girls you talk about, they would chain me to them and throw away the key. They would expect hearts and flowers and the whole relationship thing. Aunt Alice wants me to learn what it's like to date one girl until the end of the year. I must show commitment and that I'm capable of monogamy and putting someone else's needs above mine. She wants me to grow up and take responsibility for my life, but I'm not ready for that yet. When I saw you again and you reacted so strongly about my shop, I saw a way I could have it all."

Slamming my glass on the table, I stare at him angrily. "Oh, I get it. Good old Nelly. She won't cause a fuss. She won't care that it's all a show to extricate money from an elderly woman whose only wish in life is to see her family doing well. Oh no, Nelly will be so grateful to the super cool football player of her past that always got everything he wanted. Well, not this time creep face. You don't get to use me for your own twisted, sick game. I am no longer that girl at school grateful for just a kind look and a few spoken words. I've matured and grown up, something I can see you are a long way from achieving. So, the answer to your question is a big fat NO because I am not one of your simpering fans who think you pass gold when you pee. Find some other unfortunate gullible fool who doesn't class brains as a vital organ and choose Emma blooming airhead Grant instead."

I make to leave, and Jack says quickly, "I'll pay you."

CHAPTER 7

I stare at him in horror. "What did you just say?"

He looks embarrassed and says slowly, "I mean, this is a business dinner, right? Well, look on it as a business proposition. You say that my opening will ruin your business. What if I pay you, say, a year's rent, to help me out? I mean, it will only involve a few white lies and some visits to a couple of family occasions. Where's the harm in that and we could work together to make sure we both get what we want?"

I stare at him incredulously. "You're actually serious, aren't you?"

His eyes flash and he appears more determined than I have ever seen him. "I need this to work, Nelly, and you are the only girl I want to do this with."

I sit back down due to the fact my legs are shaking and whisper, "Why?"

He grins. "Because you remind me a little of Aunt Alice herself. When you stood up for yourself against Emma, I saw the fire in you that she has. You like the same things, in fact, you are already living her dream. You are beautiful, strong and clever, all the attributes she would find acceptable. With you by my side, I can't fail, which is why I'm so desperate to agree to anything if you'll only say yes."

Stupidly, all I can say is, "You think I'm beautiful?"

He smiles and says gently, "Inside and out."

I murmur, "Clever and strong?"

He grins as the waiter delivers our food, giving me some time to digest this shocking information.

I start to eat on autopilot, and he allows me the time to think about what he said.

Ok, it's not so bad. Being his girlfriend, fake or otherwise, is surely a dream come true. Not quite what I had in mind, but beggars can't be choosers. He is going to pay me, which means Chocolatti can survive another year at least. Ken gets his rent and everyone's happy. Then I think about Aunt Alice and feel bad for her. This isn't right. I mean, the poor woman is being defrauded out of her hard-earned money. It's tantamount to stealing and I will be an accomplice to fraud.

Glancing across the table, I see Jack's anxious expression and my heart melts. But this is Jack Mason. The Jack Mason. The boy I idolised my entire teenage life. How amazing it would be to introduce him as my boyfriend and rub Emma Grant's nose firmly in it. After all, he can't stray under the conditions of the will. He will be chained by my side, and I will control the situation. Me, Nelly Gray. The girl who has never controlled anything, or anyone in her life. Who knows, maybe it will be fun to call the shots?

I stare at Jack and say slowly, "How do I know you'll honour your side of the deal?"

He leans forward and says with excitement, "I'll have a contract drawn up to say I owe you a year's rent. If I back out of the deal, you can sue me. It will be signed and witnessed and completely watertight."

I resume eating and mull it over some more and by the time dessert arrives, my mind is made up. After all, Ken did tell me to embrace my inner crazy, and this is just what he meant. So, in true X-Factor style, I say sternly, "Then I have reached my decision. Draw up the contract and only once we have signed it will I agree to your frankly preposterous request."

The relief is etched across Jack's face as he reaches out once again and grasps my hand tightly.

"Thank you."

I shrug and he says with relief, "No, I really mean it. I don't think you realise just how grateful I am. Without you, I would fail, and I want you to know I'm serious about the money."

I say awkwardly. "Well, it wasn't the money that made my decision for me, if you must know."

"What did then?"

Sighing, I twist the linen napkin in my fingers and say despondently, "It was no fun being me at school. When you're the daughter of the headmaster, the expectations are high. I was never included and not just because of the way I looked. My parents created a ticking time bomb. First, their name choice, I mean, who doesn't think about every rhyming combination possible when sending their child out into the wide world? Smelly Nelly was kind of obvious when you think about it, but it still hurt. I was never included and missed out on all the fun that should have been mine throughout my schooldays. I learned to develop a thick skin, but I had all the same desires and wishes as every girl there, without the ability to make them a reality. So, when you asked me to be your girlfriend, it was the one time in my life I experienced something normal. The popular boy asking the nerdy girl out and you've got to admit, it's the stuff of dreams. However, now I know even that was tainted. Once again, it was for another purpose than wanting to get to know me, the girl who was never given a chance."

He makes to speak but I smile ruefully. "It's ok, Jack, you don't have to feel sorry for me. I'm a big girl now and used to rejection. No, the reason I said yes was because I was reminded by someone close to me that life should be a little crazy from time to time. I have never been that crazy girl and now I have a chance to do something a little reckless and wild. I want to be that girl for as long as possible, just to create a memory to lock away in my heart forever. When life returns to what it should be, for girls like me, anyway, I can take that memory out and cherish it and remember the day when I had it all. So, thank you for asking me to help you because you're right. I won't expect any hearts and flowers. I won't demand your time when you would much rather be doing something else, and I won't expect you to call or send me love notes. If you look at another girl, I won't be the jealous girlfriend and above all, I don't expect a happy ever after with you. At the end of whatever this is, we can shake hands and walk away and file the experience along with no hard feelings. So, yes, Jack, I will be your girlfriend for as long as you need me to be."

I grab my wine glass and take a large mouthful of Dutch courage, ignoring the sympathy reflected back at me from across the table. He makes to speak but I laugh lightly. "Don't say it. I don't need your words of denial or encouragement. Let's just accept this for what it really is, a brief moment in time when our lives cross paths. Now, what exactly do you want me to do?"

Jack smiles a little guiltily. "I think we just let things run their course. We'll tell our friends we have started dating. I'll take you home to meet my family and introduce you as my girlfriend. Aunt Alice will no doubt hear via the grapevine, and I will involve you in my family life at every opportunity."

I nod and then say somewhat playfully, "You do know you'll also have to meet my parents. I mean, if a job's worth doing, it's worth doing well."

I savour the sight of the blood draining from his face as he pictures a night spent with his old headmaster and then he recovers and says lightly, "Of course, that's fine. I mean, if we're going to do this, we should make it believable in every way."

Nodding, I feel the excitement return as I think about the near future. This will be interesting.

* * *

THE REST of the evening was spent discussing the finer details and Jack told me that he would start dropping my name into the conversation at home and work and I was to do the same. We must play the part of love's young dream whenever we are in public. Do I feel bad about deceiving just about the entire planet? Actually, I couldn't care less. Just for once, I intend on releasing my selfish inner devil and grab what I want with both hands.

Jack Mason and Nelly Gray, who would ever have thought?

CHAPTER 8

The next day, I open Chocolatti with a new spring in my step. Its future is guaranteed for another year, at least if all goes well and I am about to live a life that has been denied to me for so many years. Finally, I'm about to discover the joys of having an actual pretend boyfriend with none of the uncertainty that normally accompanies it. I know he won't leave me after a few dates. I won't have to worry about what is considered the respectable length of time to wait before allowing him access to my woman parts. I won't have to worry about him playing around behind my back and I won't need to make scintillating conversation just to keep him interested.

Around midday, my friend Angela heads my way and looks at me curiously. "Um… Nelly, you're not going to believe what I've just heard."

I shrug. "What?"

She laughs nervously. "It's probably just silly gossip, but the woman who works next to me said she overheard a conversation at More Than Chocolate this morning."

She rolls her eyes. "You're going to laugh at this, but apparently, she heard Jack Mason telling Emma Grant you were going out, you know, a couple."

She laughs and I shrug. "Why is that so hard to believe?"

Her hand flies to her mouth, and she gasps, "You mean it's true!"

Relishing the moment, I say airily, "It is, actually. He took me out last night and asked me again to be his girlfriend. I thought I may as well give it a shot, you know, she who dares and all that nonsense."

Angela shakes her head. "I can't believe it. You and Jack Mason. I never saw that coming."

I say smugly, "Yes, it was a surprise to me too. Anyway, what did Emma say?"

As soon as the words leave my lips, I realise you never really leave the classroom. I wish I'd been there to see her expression, but hearing about it will be just as sweet.

Angela grins. "My friend said she didn't take it well. Apparently, she thought by working in the shop it would result in their engagement. She was last seen storming into the kitchen muttering curses under her breath."

I don't have time to respond because the door chimes and as I look up, my heart flutters when I see the man himself heading my way, holding a takeaway coffee in his extremely capable hands.

He winks at Angela and then throws me the most irresistible smile. "Hey, babe. I thought you could use a coffee to keep you going. I brought you a latte, but if you prefer something else, I'll go and change it."

Savouring Angela's incredulous expression, I smile sweetly and reach out to recover the coffee. Then, to my surprise, he says in a sexy voice. "Not so fast. I've missed you today."

Then, to my utter surprise and proving that dreams do come true, he pulls me towards him and lowers his lips to mine. I don't even register that this is our first kiss as his velvet lips make contact and he kisses me so deeply I think I'm never going to come up for air. As kisses go, this one is the stuff of dreams. Not that I have many to compare it with, but in my dreams I've shared many a tongue twister with Jack Mason. He wraps his hand around my hair and pulls my head even closer. Like the shameless hussy I am, I allow him total access to my tonsils and kiss him back, relishing every flutter in my heart. Then, he pulls back and smiles sweetly, saying, "I'll look forward to continuing this after work. I'll meet you outside at five thirty. Maybe we could grab a bite to eat on the way home."

Then he rubs his thumb over my wet lips and winks before heading back to his shop.

I watch in total disbelief at his retreating figure, and I think he must have served his first customer by the time my mouth moves from the floor to join the rest of me.

Angela exhales sharply and says jealously, "That was intense. You are so lucky. I can't believe it. You're a dark horse, do you know that, Nelly Gray?"

Raising my fingers to my lips, I touch the place he was last and feel my heart beating out of control. Wow, this fake girlfriend thing has some very real benefits. I knew this was a good idea. I can't wait to get home and add this new addition to my journal to keep me warm during the wilderness years in the future.

Angela hangs around for another two hours pretending to help me in the shop when all she wants to talk about is Jack. That actually suits me fine because he is my new favourite topic of conversation.

It's only when we're sorting out the chocolate mice from the chocolate bunnies that the door opens and Emma Grant heads inside. Stifling the irritation, I glance up and say politely, "May I help you?"

She gifts me a hard look and says harshly, "Look, I don't

know what's going on here, but Jack told me you are now officially an item. Is this true?"

I take great delight in saying smugly, "Yes, it is."

She shakes her head. "Something's not right. I mean, he can't have chosen you, Nelly Gray, the headmaster's daughter. He could have anyone he chooses. Why you?"

I say in a hard voice, "Look, I am standing here and believe it or not, I do have feelings. Anyway, what's it to you who he goes out with? You're not together anymore – are you?"

Suddenly, I feel nervous. What if they are? I mean, they used to date at school, at least I think they did. What if they still have the odd um… moment and she has something of a claim on him?

She says sadly, "You're right, it's none of my business. Jack and I used to date but haven't for some time. When he opened the shop and needed staff, I jumped at the chance to work with him. We did date at school, but life got in the way – that and his out-of-control libido. We drifted apart, but I never forgot him."

She appears quite upset, and despite the fact she is my past nemesis, I find myself wanting to comfort her. Offering her one of my taster chocolates, I say kindly, "Listen, maybe this has all happened for a reason. Who knows, the perfect guy for you may be just around the corner and now you're ready to meet him, minus any complications. I'm not sure how this all happened, but it has."

She looks at me in shock and shakes her head – again. "I'm sorry, Nelly. When I saw you the other day at the opening, I was in shock. I hardly recognised you and I'm ashamed of myself. You were right to have a go at me after the hell we put you through at school. It's only now I can see things from your side. Will you forgive me, and can we start again?"

I can sense Angela's surprise beside me and I think back over all those years of hurt and rejection. I remember how her words wounded my soul and destroyed my self-worth. She made me so miserable I used to cry myself to sleep at night and beg to stay off school the next day. Now she wants forgiveness – just like that. One simple apology and I'm meant to forget the past to make her feel better.

Angela nudges me and as I look, I note the usual kind face staring back at me. Angela was no stranger to bullying and rejection, yet always managed to look on the positive side. She used to say the bullies must have hard lives outside of school and who knew what horrors they went home to? I was never as forgiving as Angela, and I can see things haven't changed. I don't want to forgive and forget. I want my pound of flesh and fully intend on ignoring Emma Grant for eternity but seeing her standing before me looking so contrite, my heart softens, and I say lightly, "Of course, it's all in the past as far as I'm concerned."

Angela sighs with relief and Emma peers at me gratefully. "Thanks, Nelly. I don't deserve your forgiveness, but I'll take it. I am sorry you know, and will try to make it up to you."

She catches sight of the clock on the wall and groans. "I need to head back. My break's over and we're fairly busy so I should go and lend a hand."

She smiles sweetly and heads to the door and then turns, saying, "You know, a group of us are heading out for a pizza tonight. You're both welcome to join us."

Angela nods, saying happily, "I'd love that. What time and where?"

Emma smiles. "Six thirty by the pizza station. Meet us there."

She turns to me. "What about you, Nelly? Are you in?"

Feeling smug, I shake my head. "Not tonight. I'm heading out with Jack after work."

Emma's face falls a little and she nods. "Of course. Maybe next time."

She smiles sweetly and heads outside and Angela exhales deeply. "Wow, that was tense. I can't believe she apologised to you. I'm proud of the way you handled that."

I watch Emma crossing the road and say, "Well, let's hope it was genuine, but be careful tonight, Angela. Old habits die hard, and I'd hate for you to get your hopes up thinking things have changed."

She rolls her eyes. "We're not in the playground now, Nelly. I think she was genuinely remorseful and probably just wants to make it up to us."

Pushing away an uneasy feeling, I smile brightly. "Of course. Who wouldn't want to be your friend? I hope you have a great night."

She nudges me. "I'd trade places with you like a shot, though. I can't believe how lucky you are. Make sure he's got a friend for me – we could double date."

Laughing, I reply, "If he has, I'll make sure to introduce you."

Angela heads home to get ready for her girly pizza date, leaving me a hot mess. Jack kissed me. Really kissed me, like in the films. I wasn't prepared for it and it took me by complete surprise. That kiss has changed everything. I want more of them and suddenly this 'relationship' has become something much more to me. If there's the slightest possibility that I could actually get Jack Mason to like me as a woman, maybe I should think about this and up my game. I have a chance here to grab something previously unattainable. The dream could come true – couldn't it?

CHAPTER 9

I'm surprised to see Jack waiting outside when I lock up for the night. Feeling a little shy after the kiss, I smile and say in a low voice. "You know, you didn't really have to meet me. We could just pretend. I mean, surely you have better things to do."

He raises his eyes and says gently, "I don't have anything better to do, as you put it. Maybe I just want to get to know my girlfriend before I introduce her to my family."

I nod shyly. "Oh, of course. We should tell each other things about each other just in case. You know, like favourite food, music, etc."

We start walking and I say with interest, "Where are we going?"

Jack smiles. "I thought it may be a good idea to check out our homes. I mean, I'd love you to come home with me and see where I live, and the same goes for me. You can tell a lot about a person from their home."

Thinking about the mess I left my flat in earlier, I shudder and say lightly, "Shall we start with yours?"

Nodding, he gestures to his car parked nearby. "Ok, it's not far. Hop in."

Jack's car is like the man himself — impressive. It's a sleek black BMW which reminds me how he always appeared to have money, even at school. I'm curious about his life and say lightly, "You appear to have it all, Jack. These cars don't come cheap."

He appears faintly embarrassed. "I suppose I have been quite lucky. My parents always had good jobs and money was never a problem. As you say, I appear to have it all."

"Then why are you so keen to get your aunt's money? Surely you have enough already."

He shrugs. "Not really. You see, I have big plans. I want to take a year out and travel. You know, to exotic places that I've only read about. Experience a bit of life before I settle down. If I ever settle down, that is."

Rolling my eyes, I say firmly, "That's where you're irresponsible. I can see why your aunt is concerned."

He smiles. "Why, exactly?"

"Well, put it this way: if you continue the way you're going, you'll be like the Hawaiian pizza on the menu."

He laughs. "Explain."

Grinning, I say cheekily, "It was popular once but now everyone's had a taste. It's still on the menu, but nobody wants it anymore."

Jack laughs so hard I worry we're about to crash. Then he says with amusement, "What kind of pizza do you like, Nelly Gray?"

Thinking for a moment, I say with feeling, "Plain old margarita, of course. You can never go wrong with that good old favourite. It's just what it says on the box, and you can always add the odd ingredient to spice it up a little. It never goes out of fashion and is the most popular item on the menu. Now your turn."

He smirks. "Americano. Hot and spicy and guaranteed to make your mouth water."

I roll my eyes and groan. "Obviously."

Jack grins and then pulls into a parking space outside an impressive block of flats. He turns off the ignition and says proudly, "Chez Jack."

I exit the car as gracefully as I can and look up at the smart building in front of me. Jack comes and stands beside me and, to my surprise, takes my hand in his. I stare at him in confusion and say "It's ok, you don't have to carry on the act when there's nobody around. As I said, this is a business arrangement, nothing else."

He lowers his voice and whispers, "You never know who may be watching. These windows hide many a prying eye and they may be called upon to give evidence."

Snatching my hand away, I say brusquely, "I doubt that. You forget I'm not the usual airhead you date. I'm actually immune to your charms and newsflash, I'm only here because you're paying me to be."

Laughing, he spins me around and smiles sexily, "So, if I kissed you now, you would hate every minute of it."

Pushing him away, I say tartly, "Once was quite enough, thank you. Now, are you going to brief me on your living conditions or just keep me outside while you practise your not so sharp seduction skills?"

I take a moment to savour the victory when I see a shadow pass across his eyes. For someone used to getting everything he wants, I'm guessing this brush off is alien to him. Feeling glad I can help him experience something the rest of us take for granted, I gaze pointedly at the building. "Lead on Macduff."

His confusion makes me laugh and he just shrugs and heads towards the communal door and lets us inside.

* * *

JACK'S APARTMENT IS IMPRESSIVE. Cool, modern, and tastefully furnished. A typical bachelor pad, which I'm guessing he has used to its full advantage.

White leather sofas sit around a beautiful, soft, grey shaggy rug. Chrome light fittings and the odd pot plant are set against white walls filled with large bold canvases. One is of a nude woman in a seductive pose, and I laugh out loud. "Goodness, could this flat be any more stereotypical?"

He appears hurt and says in a small voice, "Don't you like it?"

Now I'm ashamed of my rudeness and say warmly, "Actually, I love it. It suits you. If I could picture your home in my mind, I suppose this is what I would see. I love what you've done with it, although as a modern woman, I must object to the picture hanging on your wall."

Jack grins. "So, you're one of those."

"Excuse me?"

"A feminist."

I snap, "Just because I don't like seeing a woman naked and spread out for everyone's pleasure on the wall, it doesn't make me a feminist. I suppose I am, but not in the way you are obviously insinuating. I like equal opportunities between men and women, but I also recognise that in some things men are better than women and vice versa. For example, in our case, I am obviously better at academic pursuits than you and you are better at sports. Do I want to prove that I'm better at football than you? Of course not. Do I believe I am better than you at business? Probably, because I would never in a million years open up opposite someone and sell the same thing as them."

Jack rolls his eyes and murmurs, "That again."

I snap. "Yes, that again. It will be that again all the time you continue to sell chocolate in your shop. It will be that again, all the time you take the money from my cash register that was heading my way and it will be that again until the day you close your doors because I have worked hard to achieve my dream. I haven't had it handed to me on a plate. I had to go the usual way and plead for a loan from the bank. I had to work out a mighty watertight business plan to persuade them I was a solid investment and then I had to spend the small budget I had to fit out the shop in IKEA and then customise the fixtures. You see, Jack, I have had to work extremely hard for everything, unlike you, who appears to have opened on a whim."

I'm almost out of breath and the adrenalin runs high as my breath comes fast and furiously. I feel my cheeks are flushed and my eyes bright with anger as I dwell on the injustice in life. Then I notice that Jack is looking at me strangely and I feel bad. My shoulders sag and I say apologetically, "I'm sorry. I didn't mean to vent like that. The trouble is, it's been so hard to get where I am, I'm feeling quite vulnerable at the moment."

He says gently, "Take a seat and I'll fix you a drink. Perhaps we should just chill for a while. What do you prefer, white wine or maybe a spritzer?"

I say quietly, "I wouldn't mind a cup of tea."

He raises his eyes. "Seriously, tea!"

I say in a hard voice, "What's wrong with that? We're not all alcoholics, you know. Let me guess, your usual guests probably sit perched on this seat with their chest forwards and their eyes swimming with an invitation. I can just hear them now. Oh yes, Jack, a lovely white wine would be amazing. Let's take it to bed."

I grin as he laughs out loud and says, "You've done this before."

My eyes flash. "Is that what you think? That I'm just like them?"

He shakes his head. "You are nothing like them, I can assure you. Well, a cup of tea it is, milady."

He bows and despite myself, I grin. This is actually a lot of fun. Educating Jack Mason in the fact that not every girl is after him is a satisfying experience.

CHAPTER 10

I sink back and relax against the comfortable cushions and even kick off my shoes and tuck my legs underneath me as I sprawl on his designer couch. Looking around, I could picture myself in a place like this. All mod cons and designer isms. This is what I want; if I had this, I would think I'd made it.

Catching sight of the picture, I wonder if I could change it for one of a sexy man instead. Yes, that would be nice, eye candy to add fuel to my fantasies. We would be a couple and I would talk to him about my hopes and dreams. He would never answer back, which makes him the perfect man, for me, anyway. I almost forget I'm in Jack's apartment, as my dream becomes a reality. I practice my smug expression and blow kisses to my imaginary boyfriend on the wall. I stretch sexily on the couch and practice looking at ease in my surroundings. Then I'm aware that Jack is watching me with a quizzical expression as he heads back into the room, holding two mugs of steaming tea. Ignoring his amusement, I hold out my hand and say primly, "Thank you."

He sits beside me way too close, and I start feeling a bit hot and edging away, I laugh nervously. "So, how long have you lived here?"

He shifts a little closer. "Eight months."

My voice is a little high as I say, "So, this is your bachelor pad, then. Do you live alone?"

He leans towards me and my breath hitches. "Not always."

I squeak. "What's that supposed to mean?"

He winks. "It depends on who I'm seeing at the time. Sometimes they stay over for the weekend and sometimes just the night."

I stand and move across to the window and say sarcastically, "That doesn't surprise me. So, how are you going to cope with having a girlfriend, or should I say pretend one? I mean, it's obvious you're used to entertaining on a regular basis. Will that continue? I mean, I don't really care, but as you said yourself, you need to prove you can commit."

He stands and, moving beside me, says in a low voice, "Maybe I like a challenge and maybe I want to be more than just pretend with you."

In a voice higher than any opera singer, I say nervously, "In your dreams. What would that say about me? No, this is a business arrangement, nothing more, nothing less. Maybe you haven't thought this through properly."

He laughs softly. "I've thought about everything, Nelly. Trust me, I have it all worked out."

Flashing him a nervous smile, I head back and grab my tea, my heart pounding relentlessly inside me. This is different. I've never been in this situation before and it's strange. On the one hand, I'm quite keen to develop this friend with benefits vibe he has going on, but I am kind of protective over my heart and know this is all a game to him. He's just playing me like the player he is. I'm not strong enough to join in because I know I'd be the one bearing the scars from this experience. So, I just smile weakly and change the subject.

"So, tell me about your family. What do you think they'll make of all this?"

"They are in it with me."

He sighs. "Aunt Alice is a conniving woman, and I'm not the only one in her will. My family has their own challenges and it's shaken things up enormously."

I lean forward with interest. "What are their challenges?"

He grins and I try to focus on his words rather than his delectable mouth as he speaks.

"Well, my parents have a joint challenge. They must learn salsa dancing and enter a competition. It doesn't matter if they win, they just have to give it their best shot."

I stare at him in disbelief. "That's not so bad, surely."

He smiles wickedly. "It's the worst thing possible for them. They can't stand each other and haven't for years. They do everything they can to avoid one another and now they will have to spend an obscene amount of time together – in their eyes, anyway. Any normal couple would relish the chance. However, as I'm sure you'll quickly discover, they are far from normal."

Thinking of my own parents and how happy they have always been, I struggle to imagine a home where the parents hate each other.

Jack must sense my sympathy because he shakes his head. "Don't feel sorry for me. It's taught me a thing or two about relationships, which is why I won't make the same mistake myself. No, I'm going to be selfish for as long as possible because marriage, in my eyes, taints your soul. If my parents had a choice, they would have split years ago, but they are so deeply involved in one another's lives, it would be a messy business."

I'm shocked and am beginning to understand a little of what makes Jack Mason tick. I still don't agree with his viewpoint on life and relationships, but then again, I've never had to endure a warring family like him.

Shaking any sympathetic thoughts away, I say lightly, "Is there anyone else, brothers or sisters perhaps?"

He nods. "Ariadne, my sister. She has the worst one of all."

I gaze at him with interest, and he grins. "When you meet my sister, you'll understand why this is so difficult for her. You think I'm spoiled? Well, you're about to hand the crown to someone else. Namely my sister, princess 'I want it all.' She is spoiled and rude and gets everything she wants. Her whole day is taken up with posing for Instagram pictures and shopping. Her boyfriend was selected according to his bank balance and ability to indulge her every whim. She is cosseted and vain, which is why her task is all the sweeter."

I can't stand the suspense and say pleadingly, "What does she have to do?"

He grins. "Work in a care home for the rest of the year."

"Is that it? What's so bad about that?"

"You'll see. Anyway, now you know, that's the Masons. Vain, conceited and so wrapped up in their own selfish ways, it's no wonder my aunt has put her foot down."

I think about what he's said. They sound positively awful, and I would hate to belong to a family like that.

He leans forward and says with interest. "Your turn. I know you're the headmaster's daughter, but what about your home life? Is it as bad as we all thought?"

I feel myself bristling. "For your information, my parents are fantastic people. I had a very happy childhood and I respect them immensely. I also have a sister who is studying at Oxford. Any spare time she has, she volunteers with the local charity."

Jack appears shocked and I shrug. "What's the matter? Not normal enough for you?"

He shakes his head and looks contrite. "I'm not judging you,

Nelly. I suppose I'm a little fascinated, really. My folks don't have much time for us and just think shoving money at a problem will make it go away. This flat we're in, they bought it. I expect they wanted to get rid of me, so I wouldn't witness their constant fighting and question their dubious timekeeping."

"What do you mean?"

He sighs. "They may live in the same house, but they socialise in a very different way. They think I don't know, but I've heard the rumours and the fights over the years. They like to play the field and have become less discreet lately. Both Ariadne and I know the score, and if they split up, it would probably be a blessing. Their marriage is on a knife's edge, and it will only take one final slip to sever the connection for good."

To my own surprise, I place my hand on his knee and smile softly. He looks startled as I say sadly, "I'm sorry, it must be difficult seeing that."

He lowers his eyes. "It is. I put on a brave face, but it still hurts. It's no wonder I have commitment issues after watching them over the years."

He rests his hand over mine and I drown in his dark brown eyes, that have softened into liquid pools of melted chocolate. He says gently, "Thank you for being here. I don't know why, but it's as if I can tell you anything. You won't judge me, and I know any secret I share with you will be in safe hands."

I nod, feeling a little of my resolve slipping away. "You can count on me, Jack. I told you that and won't let you down."

Just for a moment, we sit in companionable silence, hand in hand, on Jack's white settee. Now he has let a little of his façade slip, I peer behind the cocky popular boy from school and see an insecure young man who is still searching for himself in the middle of a storm that I find myself wanting to help him navigate through. Who knows, maybe if we are successful, he should see the world and grow as an individual? There's no law that we all must conform to type and marry and have kids as a matter of duty. Maybe he does have the right idea after all, and maybe I should let go of a little of my own reserve and see where it takes me.

So, for the rest of the evening, we order take out and chat like old friends. The wall I was hiding behind has shifted and now I can open up to him and discover we share a lot in common.

By the time Jack drops me home, I have thawed a little towards him. Then, as I make to exit the car, he pulls me back and says softly, "Will you let me kiss you, Nelly?"

My heart starts beating rapidly and I wonder what the right answer is here. However, my desire places my reasoning in a headlock, and I say shyly, "For appearance's sake only, of course."

His eyes sparkle as he smiles triumphantly. "Yes, of course. For appearance's sake only."

He reaches across and wraps his hand around the back of my head and pulls me towards him. Then I hold my breath as he lowers his lips to mine and kisses me softly and sweetly. His touch is gentle and causes my heart to flutter. He strokes the side of my face with his fingers and entwines my tongue in his. I feel wanted, cherished and desired and it's the first time in my life I ever have. No rushed wet kiss from an inexperienced boy who lunges in for the kill. No tongue sucking marathon by a boy who never learned the skill involved. No, this is a tiny taste of heaven executed by an experienced man. The man I always lusted after and dreamed of in bed at night. So, what if it's fake. I'm a woman, after all, and it's no hardship feeling his attention.

As he pulls back, his eyes sparkle as he whispers, "I'll see you in the morning. Thanks for a great evening. Maybe tomorrow we can spend the evening at your flat."

Words fail me, so I just nod before exiting the car. As I walk back to my apartment, I can still feel the imprint of his lips on mine. I walk on a cloud and it's only when I turn the key in the lock and see the familiar waiting for me that I realise what's happening and, leaning back against the door in shock, I shake my head at my own stupidity.

Just for a minute, I dared to dream. I never stopped wanting Jack Mason and as sure as he's going to walk away from me at the end of this once his aunt's cheques is deposited in his bank, I'm about to get my heart shattered into a million pieces because I love Jack Mason and I always have.

CHAPTER 11

The next day, I sense the nerves returning. Tonight, Jack wants to visit my flat, and it's nothing compared to his. I woke up early and did my best to tidy up and make it look better than it is, but there's only so much you can do with obvious second-hand furniture and more mess than a person has any right to accumulate.

I feel quite despondent, and my mood doesn't improve when the first thing I see is a flirtatious Jack laughing with a group of giggling girls, who are already sitting outside his shop.

He doesn't see me, and I feel strangely annoyed to see him so obviously flirting. I shouldn't be. After all, he's been open from the start. He's not looking for a real girlfriend when there are obviously so many women clamouring for his attention.

So, as usual, I resort to eating my stock as soon as I set foot inside my shop and stalk him in the spy mirror, getting more despondent as the day goes on. The only light relief is when Richie pays me a visit and I fill him in on what's been happening – the official version, at least.

"Oh. My. God. You lucky cow."

I raise my eyes and he grins. "Whoever said dreams don't come true was so wrong. Wait until I tell Roger."

I roll my eyes. "Is it that much of a surprise? After all, surely he's the lucky one in all this."

Richie's eyes soften and he gives me a hug. "Of course, he's the lucky one. Any guy would be. I mean, you are totally the full package, and any guy would think he had it all with you beside him."

I laugh self-consciously. "Well, you would say that because you're my friend. Anyway, how are things at home?"

He shrugs. "Dreadful. If I hear one more gory detail about that knee operation, I'm liable to crack and break his other one just to give myself some respite while he does another stint in the hospital. I'm even contemplating fabricating a trip away to get out of going home. I've started looking up mini breaks for one on the web and was that close to booking a trip to Tenerife yesterday when he started moaning about the pain and could I just plump his cushions a little more."

I frown and say firmly. "You should have a little more compassion; he must be in agony."

Richie shakes his head. "Only when I'm looking. I saw him yesterday when he thought I was out. He was dancing to Ed Sheeran and his knee looked fine then. When I slammed the front door, he fell on the settee and started groaning, saying he needed me to bring him some medicinal brandy for the pain. Quite honestly, Nelly, that man's a monster, and I'm so going to get my revenge."

"Why? What are you going to do?"

"I'm not sure, but you can rest assured it will involve lots of pain for him – of the mental kind."

Grinning, I look up as Angela heads inside and glances at me sheepishly. Instantly, the alarm bells start ringing and I say brightly, "Hi, how was your evening with the popular crowd?"

She smiles happily. "Actually, I really enjoyed it. Emma was nicer than I thought and really included me. Madison was also so funny, and I never realised how nice they really are."

Richie looks interested. "Then why the face?"

"Excuse me."

"The face. You came in here looking like you had something on your mind, and we want to know what?"

She sighs heavily and appears a little worried. "I'm sorry. It's just that they said things about Jack, and it made me uncomfortable."

I try to look uninterested but say quickly, "Like what?"

She sighs. "Emma told me that he's such a raging flirt. He flirts with all their customers and girls are always giving him their phone numbers. Apparently, when they went out, he was talking to several other girls at the time, and she went through his phone and found explicit texts to several other women. She said he's the unfaithful type and they pity you."

I shrug. "So what? That's in the past. He's grown up since then and if that's what he wants to do, it's up to him. We're not married or anything. I mean, say a fit guy came in here and gave me his number – I'd take it. We've only been dating for two days. It's hardly serious."

Angela smiles sympathetically and Richie looks thoughtful. "Yes, if he's a player, it kind of goes with the territory."

We stare across the road and observe Jack leaning over a group of girls and laughing at something one of them says. Fighting back the irritation, I say bluntly, "I'm not going to be the jealous girlfriend. He's an entrepreneur and is establishing his business. Being nice to the customers is the number one rule, and a bit of playful banter isn't going to hurt anyone. However, it was me who spent the evening with him and will do again tonight."

Richie says with interest. "Ooh, tell us all the gory details."

I just smirk like the cat who got the cream and say mysteriously, "All in good time, my good friend."

I turn my attention to Angela. "So, you enjoyed your evening then?"

She nods with excitement. "Yes, they've invited me to the cinema tonight. We're seeing that new chick-flick with Zac Efron. What I wouldn't give to go out with a guy like that."

Richie sighs. "You'd have to fight me off first, darling. Anyway, I need to go and plan my revenge. I'm going to grab a coffee across the street and observe this philandering boyfriend for myself. If I don't like what I see, I'll pretend my coffee's cold and object at the top of my voice. Let's see how his customer care skills work then."

Laughing, we watch him head off and Angela sighs. "You know, whatever they say, you're still lucky. I hope I find Mr Right soon. I want some of what you're having because I've never seen you looking so radiant."

I raise my hand to my face and say with surprise. "I don't look any different. What do you mean?"

She laughs softly. "You do, Nelly. Your face looks different somehow. Like you have that love look."

"Love look?"

Giggling, Angela pulls me over to the spy mirror. "Look, your eyes are bright and your cheeks glowing. You appear happy and satisfied, and I am so jealous right now."

Shaking my head, I say with amusement. "You're silly. I don't look any different. Anyway, I must get to work because I have a chocolate rep due, and I must take stock of what I need."

As I catch sight of Jack in the mirror, I notice him taking a piece of paper from one of the girls who is openly flirting with him. Even from here, I see the loaded look they share, and my irritation threatens to blow this whole charade wide open. However, I can see a way of getting my own back on Jack and say to Angela, "I'm not sure if you've got the time, but can you look after the shop for me when my rep arrives?"

She nods. "Of course. How long do you need?"

"Oh, about an hour at the most. That will be perfect."

CHAPTER 12

Ten minutes later, the door chimes and I look up to see my favourite rep heading through the door. Gary is quite easy on the eye and a terrible flirt, rivalling Jack Mason in that department with ease.

He winks as he heads inside and says in a loud voice, "How's my favourite customer today?"

Knowing this is just sales talk, I smile happily. "Hey, Gary, how's my favourite rep?"

He winks and places his case on the floor in front of the counter. "All the better for seeing you, Nelly. Now, is there a cup of tea with my name on it, or do I have to go and make it myself?"

I giggle at the expression on Angela's face. She is spellbound because Gary is cocky, confident, and extremely good looking.

She blushes as he turns his attention to her. "Who do we have here, then? Your new sexy assistant, by the looks of things."

She blushes as I grin. "Yes, Gary, meet Angela. She likes men who know what they want and foreign holidays."

Angela throws me a mortified look and I giggle as Gary

reaches out and takes her hand in his, kissing the back of it gallantly. "Well, I'm pleased to meet you, gorgeous Angela."

He turns his attention back to me and I'm no fool. This is Gary's sales patter, which is why I completely overspend with him. He is the number one rep in the business because he charms the pants off all his customers, making them feel as if they are the most special ones in the world. Today he is going to be my weapon in teaching Jack Mason another lesson, so I smile sweetly. "Let's take our meeting over the road. It's a lovely day and we can grab a coffee in the new shop. You know, the guy who opened it is a total sleaze. He actually has the gall to sell chocolate in there. Can you imagine doing something so underhand?"

Gary shakes his head. "Shocking, babe. Let's go and suss out the competition and you can rest assured he will not be getting his money hungry hands on any of my chocolates. I'm loyal to my favourite customers, so let's go and check this creep out."

Smiling our goodbyes to Angela, we head across the road and take a seat outside More Than Chocolate.

As Gary puts down his cases, Jack appears and says with surprise, "Hi Nelly, this is an unexpected treat. What can I get you? On the house, of course."

Gary pretends to gag behind his back, and I smile brightly. "A latte for me and what will you have, Gary?"

He glares at Jack and says frostily, "A flat white please."

Jack looks surprised and then frowns as I smile flirtatiously at Gary and say dismissively. "Thanks, Jack."

Gary removes a catalogue from his case, effectively demoting Jack to the hired help and says forcefully, "Right then, babe. It's time for you to fleece me for everything I've got."

He winks and I notice Jack's expression harden, but he has no choice but to walk away.

Gary is a good rep for a reason and has sussed out the situation perfectly. He flirts outrageously with me the entire time and pops many delicious samples of chocolate in my mouth, while I groan loudly, savouring the delicious taste. It becomes a bit like 'When Nelly met Gary' and I totally overplay the orgasm scene. I see many interested looks thrown our way and one very irritated one. Gary plays his part to perfection and there is so much giggling and flirtatious behaviour that even I begin to believe it a little.

Every so often, I witness Jack looking daggers at Gary and feel the smug sense of revenge as he totally gets a taste of his own medicine. Emma watches with amusement, and I can tell she is finding it hard to keep a straight face. After one particularly satisfying groan, Jack rushes over and says frantically, "Can I get you anything else?"

Gary throws me a look that would melt every chocolate in my shop and says sexily, "I think we're good, thanks. You know, Nelly is my favourite customer for a reason. She certainly knows how to savour the finer things in life."

He winks, and I giggle like a schoolgirl. "Oh, Gary, you know you're my favourite rep too. Nobody else has the same… um… passion for what they do. You know, maybe we should continue this meeting back at the shop. Jack will probably need the table and we can finish this… um… in private."

Gary reaches out and grabs my hand and says gruffly, "Yes, let's take this inside and seal the deal."

He winks suggestively and Jack's frown almost makes me laugh out loud.

As Gary gathers his things, Jack pulls me to one side and hisses, "What are you doing?"

I smile innocently. "Having a business meeting."

He says angrily. "No, you're not, you're flirting with him and he's taking advantage of it."

I shrug. "We all must do what's necessary in business, Jack. I'm sure you are not averse to using your attraction capabilities to squeeze a little more from your customers. We all do it. It doesn't mean anything, after all."

Shaking off his hand, I smile at Gary and say in a low, husky voice. "Here, let me carry your sack of goodies."

Gary winks and I giggle, leaving Jack with a face like thunder, as we head back to Chocolatti.

As we stumble back into the shop, Angela glances up with interest. "What's so funny?"

Gary grins. "I love coming here. You're such fun, Nelly. When you started groaning, I thought I'd lose it."

Angela says in confusion. "Groaning?"

I laugh softly. "Yes, Jack's discovered he's not the only one who can flirt like a pro. Maybe it might just teach him a thing or two."

We settle down and do what we should have done an hour ago, and I make sure to place a larger order than normal. As Gary prepares to leave, he smiles at us both and says sweetly, "Thanks for an enjoyable morning. I wish my afternoon was going to be as exciting, but I have the customer from hell waiting. He just eats all my samples and then tells me he doesn't need anything and to give him a call next week."

Angela looks shocked. "That's terrible. Tell him he can't have a taste unless he commits to an order."

Gary grins at her, making her blush. "It doesn't work like that, but I'll take your advice on board. Hopefully, when I come next time, I'll report back and say your advice worked."

He says softly, "I'll look forward to it, Angela."

Rolling my eyes, I see him to the door and say gratefully, "Thanks, Gary, for everything. Hopefully, that's shown Jack I'm not to be messed around with."

He laughs softly. "Jack's your boyfriend, isn't he?"

"How do you know?"

"Because he was throwing me evil looks the entire time I was there. He couldn't take his eyes off you and every time you laughed, or groaned, I might add, he got this nervous tick in his jaw. I watched him the whole time, and he was all over the place. Well, good for you, Nelly. Don't let guys like that mess you around when there are so many more out there. Anyway, I should go, but tell me one thing before I do."

"What?"

"Is Angela seeing anyone?"

Grinning, I whisper, "No, but don't you go breaking her heart, otherwise I'll set my boyfriend on you."

He throws a hot look in Angela's direction and says sweetly, "We're not all players, you know. I may talk the talk, but I walk a very different kind of walk."

He leaves the shop laughing and I raise my eyes. Men!

CHAPTER 13

When I meet up with Jack later, I face him with newfound confidence. I have started to realise that two can play at this game and because I'm not really in this for love; I am going to make it my mission to teach him a valuable lesson. However, then I remember we're heading back to my flat tonight and the nerves pull me back into line because Jack will soon see that where he has nearly everything, I have next to nothing.

However, I'm the one who is surprised because he meets me apparently worried. "Hey, Nelly, I'm sorry about tonight, but I need to visit my parents. They're insisting on a visit because I haven't touched base with them since the grand opening. Mum has made her signature spag bol and told me I must bring my new girlfriend."

I stare at him in shock. "How do they know about me already?"

He grins sheepishly. "I think I bragged a little when they called. I kind of played things up a bit and, of course, mum's sceptical."

"But won't they know this all a façade, anyway? I mean, they must know what your challenge is and if anything, they will think badly of me for agreeing to it."

He smiles softly. "To be honest, I told them that as luck would have it, I found you at the same time and had always wanted to go out with you. Subsequently, mum is super excited because I've never brought a girl home before and told my father she thinks you're the one."

I shake my head in bewilderment. "For goodness' sake, Jack, why didn't you just tell them the truth? Surely, they will understand. It doesn't make sense."

He shrugs. "I did it for you. I didn't want them to think badly of you if they found out about our arrangement. Also, it would look more realistic to Aunt Alice when we meet up at family gatherings. Mum will talk about you, as she would any girl I brought home, and it will be all the more believable."

I stare at him in surprise. "You did it for me?"

He nods, looking worried.

"Are you angry?"

Shaking my head, I say in a whisper. "How could I be angry at that? You really lied to your parents to spare my feelings?"

He nods and I smile shakily. "I don't believe it. Nobody's ever considered my feelings before. I suppose I'm so used to being trodden on and discounted I've never actually had anyone put me first before. Thank you, Jack."

He appears concerned and says softly, "You don't have to thank me, Nelly. Since meeting you, it's made me think about what I was like in the past and I don't like what I see. It's made me realise the repercussions of my actions and I feel ashamed of how we all treated you. Now I know you a little, I see that you're a kind, considerate, clever, funny, beautiful woman and I should have seen that before, but I never looked."

I don't know what to say and feel myself blushing furiously as I try to cover up how touched I am. Then I say nervously,

"So, we're heading to meet your parents. You could have warned me. I look terrible."

His eyes soften and I see why he's so successful with the ladies. He has this ability to make any girl feel as if she's the most important one in the world with just one look alone.

He takes my hand and says sincerely, "I think you look amazing. You always do. Don't worry about my parents, they may be selfish, but they aren't ogres. They'll make you feel welcome, and you can understand why I have come to the conclusions I have for my own life."

Once again, I follow Jack to his car, trying to suppress the nerves that are fluttering around inside me.

Meeting the parents – already. I'm not sure I'm ready for this.

CHAPTER 14

As I expected, Jack's family live in one of the more desirable parts of town. He pulls up in front of an impressive townhouse that appears to be arranged over four floors. The place looks immaculate from the outside and the cars parked in the driveway are the newest models and cost more than I make in a year.

Jack groans. "I'm not ready for this."

"For what?"

"For you to meet them – my family."

"Why, are you ashamed of me or something?"

I feel a mixture of anger and anxiety about his answer, but he laughs dully. "Of them."

"You're ashamed of them?"

He nods. "They're hardly the textbook parents from the rule book. I almost think they only had us to keep up appearances. All our lives, my sister and I have just been an inconvenience and were wheeled out when the occasion dictated it to make them look good."

His words make me pity him, which surprises me when I think about how much I envied him at school. Angela's words are ringing very true when she felt sympathy for the bullies. Maybe there is something in that theory. Perhaps he was dismissive because that's all he knew.

He shakes himself and says wearily, "Ok, let's get this over with."

Feeling a little worried, I follow him inside the impressive house and look around me in awe. As places go, this one is amazing and could be a spread in a fashion magazine. This is how I imagined the wealthy to live. I've seen houses like this on Pinterest and have drooled at the sight of the sumptuous furnishings with no expense spared. Jack's home is no exception because this house looks as if it has never been lived in. If a family live here, they are meticulously tidy. There is not a speck of dirt or dust and even the cushions look new and plump, as if nobody ever sits on them. The air is scented with expensive reed diffusers and I'm afraid to breathe in case I contaminate the air with real life.

Jack's smile is strained, and I hate the worry in his eyes as he drags me towards the kitchen.

I hear movement inside and the aroma that greets me makes my stomach growl. The first person I see is a beautiful woman wearing a Cath Kidston apron, stirring a pot of something that smells like pure heaven.

She glances up as we head inside the room and her eyes zoom in on me, assessing me from head to toe. I'm sure she misses nothing. Not the slightly messy ponytail I've been wearing all day because my hair could do with a wash. She must see that my make-up wore off hours ago and I have the beginnings of a spot on my nose. She must blanch at the sight of my faded jeans and t-shirt emblazoned with the name of my business, and I'm sure the sneer on her lips is directed at the chain store trainers I threw on this morning because they are my comfortable friends.

Then again, maybe she dislikes seeing her son's hand

planted firmly in mine where it has absolutely no right to be and my heart sinks. However, in a split second, she changes and smiles brightly. "Jack, darling, good of you to make it and this must be–?"

She chews on her bottom lip as if she is having trouble remembering and I say a little too brightly, "Nelly Gray. I'm pleased to meet you, Mrs Mason."

She laughs and I swear it's the sweetest sound in the world as she purses her perfect lips that are painted in the most professional manner. "Call me Amanda, my dear. Mrs Mason makes me sound so old, and I like to think I have a few more years left in me before I deserve that title."

I smile as Jack says irritably, "Where's dad?"

I note a shadow pass across her face as she sighs irritably. "Who knows, darling? He never informs me of his comings and goings these days. Maybe you should call him once in a while. You may get more sense out of him than I ever do."

Jack heads across to the fridge and grabs a couple of beers before turning to me and saying. "Beer, Nelly?"

I note the raised eyebrow stirring the pot and say lightly, "No thank you. Do you have anything softer?"

His mother says firmly, "Honestly, Jack, where are your manners? Girls aren't beer drinkers; you should know that. Offer Nelly some white wine, or a spritzer. That is much more suitable."

I smile in defeat. "That sounds lovely, thank you."

I detect a little disappointment in his eyes as he shrugs and sets about making the drink.

His mother rolls her eyes. "Men. Honestly, they know nothing about what a woman really wants. My husband's a good example. We've been married for over twenty years, and he still doesn't know what I like. At Christmas he gives me money to buy 'something nice' as he puts it. On my birthday, he resorts to flowers and a meaningless piece of jewellery and I'm pretty sure his secretary organises those."

She turns to Jack and says firmly. "Don't be like your father, be the better man. Discover what Nelly likes, I mean, really likes, and make it your mission to deliver it to her gift wrapped. No girl likes to feel like a chore, which is what married life does for you. It rips out all the passion in a relationship and replaces it with drudgery. It's all very well at the beginning when everything's new and exciting, but the shine soon fades, and the irritations of everyday life get in the way. Twenty-plus years I've been living under that domestic cloud, and I want better for Nelly here."

I am mortified hearing his mother lay her cards on the table like this. It's uncomfortable, to say the least, and I wish we hadn't come.

The door slams and I watch Amanda frown at the sound of something hitting the hall table outside. I glance up as an older version of Jack enters the room and my breath hitches. This must be his father, because he is the spitting image of him. He's wearing a tailored suit and appears immaculate and successful. He has a smattering of grey hair at the temples but is clean shaven and exudes charisma. He notices me gaping at him and smiles. "Well, hello. You must be…"

Jack says quickly. "Nelly. Her name's Nelly."

His father nods. "Of course, I remember now. Such an unusual name in the modern world."

He turns to his wife and nods. Yes, nods. No perfunctory kiss, no shared look of affection, just a curt nod. She, in turn, rolls her eyes and says wearily, "How many more times must I tell you to hang your keys up on the hook by the door? You'll mark that table in the hallway the way you slam them down. In fact, I noticed a scratch there just the other day. Really, James, you should be more careful."

I feel uncomfortable as he totally ignores her and rips off

his tie and drapes it over the nearby chair. He also heads straight for the fridge and pours himself a large glass of tonic water before grabbing a nearby bottle of gin and adding much more than a single measure to it. I watch in fascination as he removes a tray from the freezer and adds some perfect ice cubes with pieces of lemon frozen inside them. Then I watch with fascination as he downs the drink in one and says with relief, "I needed that."

Amanda makes that sound that women do when they want to convey their disapproval and he says cheerily, "I'll head off and change into something more comfortable. When's supper ready?"

I watch as Amanda stirs the pot furiously and says tightly, "Twenty minutes."

He leaves the room without another word and doesn't even look in her direction while Amanda turns her attention back to her cooking.

Jack catches my eye as he shakes his head and then says loudly, "We'll be in the living room."

Amanda says nothing, and I wonder if she's even listening as Jack drags me along with him.

CHAPTER 15

The living room is as impressive as the rest of the house and Jack pulls me beside him onto a white leather couch with extremely plump cushions and sighs. "I hope I'm never like that, Nelly."

Agreeing with him in my mind, I say gently, "I'm sure you won't be. If anything, you'll probably overcompensate for it and be that annoying husband who comes in and annoys the hell out of his family. I can imagine you like that, Jack. Cheeky, irritating and sarcastic and the most annoying husband and father."

He laughs softly. "How do you know me so well already? Let me tell you how you'll be. I bet you'll be strict and insist on proper table manners and every day will be a different meal calculated on its nutritional content and health benefits. Your children must do their homework before they can watch television and I'm certain video games and electronic devices will be rationed to one hour a night. I'm guessing your home will be run with military precision and nothing will be left to chance."

I push him angrily. "Ouch, that hurts. You know nothing

about me, just the impression you formed from those days in the classroom. For all you know, I might not want kids. I may want to become a belly dancer and run off to the desert. I could turn to prostitution now I've had my first job and I might be a gambler and win the lottery. Who knows, I may marry a prince, or live alone forever with just twenty-five cats for company. However, if I was lucky enough to be a mother, I would be the best one ever and any rules I make will be in my children's best interests."

He appears thoughtful. "What about your husband? What sort of life would he have?"

I grin. "I would be the best wife a man could wish for. I would be that wife who held everything together, in a sexy way, of course. He would idolise me because of the imaginative ways I kept him interested. He would want for nothing and yet crave everything. He would bend over backwards to do everything I tell him because I would rule him with sex."

Jack laughs out loud. "Is that a fact?"

I grin. "Yes, sex is the secret to a good marriage, and I would study the art well. My life would be dedicated to being the perfect wife and mother and I would expect no less from my husband. He would enjoy spending time with his family because he would want that more than anything. We would be a team and there would be no secrets between us. You see, I believe in soul mates, Jack, and am prepared to wait for mine to show himself. I have high standards and will not settle for less."

Laughing, he nudges me, and I grin, feeling the tension ebb away slowly. This is what's needed. Some gentle teasing to diffuse an awkward situation. I'm quite enjoying myself because I can say and do anything I want because it doesn't matter what he thinks of me. There is no anxiety over how to impress him and no watching what I say. With Jack, I can be myself because it's one hundred per cent certain that Jack isn't my soulmate and I'm not his. We will be good friends, nothing

WHEN CUPID MISSED

more, although if he throws in the odd panty-melting kiss here and there, I will not complain.

The door slams and we hear voices approaching and Jack groans. "Prepare yourself. Ariadne's here."

I hear loud voices coming from the kitchen, but can't make out what they're saying. Then I glance up with interest as two people head into the room. I smile as the girl peers at me with curiosity and smiles sweetly. "Oh, hi."

I return the smile and Jack says in a bored voice. "Nelly, this is Ariadne, my sister."

I smile shyly and don't miss the way her gaze takes me in and judges me in seconds. She is probably finding me lacking because this girl is immaculate. I'm pretty sure she has a membership to the local beauty shop because not an inch of her isn't groomed to perfection. I'm guessing she must be about eighteen and I guess to be about a size six - something I never knew actually existed in the real world. Her hair is bleached blonde and the padding in her bra gives the illusion of a centrefold hiding underneath the tight-fitting, probably cashmere, pink cropped jumper that accentuates that amazing chest. I'm not sure if she has extensions in her hair, but she definitely does on her nails. Painted to match her clothing, they reveal she has never lifted a finger for anything in her life. Her jeans look sprayed on and are ripped in that designer way that costs more than a month's salary, and her make-up is a mask that disguises the real beauty behind it.

Everything about Ariadne appears fake and when she speaks, I notice that also goes for her impressive set of veneers that look as if she never ate anything that would stain that million-dollar smile.

Behind her must be her boyfriend, who is just as bad. His hair is that floppy sort that bounces on top of his head and could do with a tub of gel to control it. He is clean shaven, and his clothes are fresh out of a movie. Chinos with a button-down shirt and pink jumper, casually tied around his neck with a smart blazer, finishing the look. They complement each other perfectly and then the illusion speaks in a breathy, girly voice, saying, "I'm sorry, I don't think we've met."

Feeling even more like Stig of the Dump, I try not to let the nerves show and say brightly, "I'm Nelly, you must be Ariadne."

She nods and appears puzzled, as if she's trying to work out what planet I'm from. Her gaze swings to Jack and I don't miss the derision in her eyes as they share a look perfected over years of living together as brother and sister. I don't like that look. I've seen it too many times in the past and know it well. Amusement followed by disapproval. A judgemental look that shows I don't measure up and never will. I'm not one of them and never will be. I'm the ugly duckling on a lake full of swans and to say my feathers are ruffled is an understatement.

It feels kind of awkward until her boyfriend steps forward with a cocky smile on his lips and holds out his hand. "I'm pleased to meet you, Nelly. I'm Godfrey, but you can call me God."

They laugh at the joke he obviously uses all the time, and I instantly dislike him. Cocking my head to one side, I say sweetly. "I'm sorry, Godfrey, that must have been a cross to bear growing up."

There's a stunned silence as they stare at me as if I'm an alien and Jack laughs loudly beside me. "Good one, Nelly."

Ariadne's cheeks turn pink and she narrows her eyes. "Yes, names are so important. I'm guessing you've had a hard time with yours over the years. Not a popular name, really, is it? It's not even chic and fashionable like mine, so bad luck on that score."

She takes Godfrey's hand and says in a girly voice. "Come on, darling. I need to update my Instagram feed and could do with your skill with the light-room app."

Without another word, they leave the room and Jack laughs softly beside me. "See what I mean?"

I nod. "I think I do. Your sister will hate what life in a care home involves. I kind of like your aunt already."

Shifting to face him, I whisper. "What does your mother do? You said she has a good job."

He rolls his eyes. "Sort of. Mum is one of those women who stays at home and keeps house. That means organising a maid service, gardeners and a window cleaner. She, in the meantime, keeps up her membership at the local country club and indulges her credit card on a daily basis. She has her tennis lessons to keep her in gossip because it's just an excuse to indulge in a glass of champagne after an arduous lesson with her friends, while they discuss their next beauty treatment."

I stare at him in confusion. "But you said she has a good job."

He smirks. "Listen, my mum is no stranger to wealth. Her family started Viapower and they've always had lots of money. The company is now in her name and she's the chairman of the board. My father's the CEO and runs everything on her behalf. They stay with each other because it suits them. He gets to play at being the boss and she trusts him to look after her parents' company. If they split, she would have to step up and he would lose his lavish lifestyle. It's more a marriage of convenience than anything else and has been for some time."

I take his hand in mine and give it a gentle squeeze. "I'm sorry."

He shrugs. "Don't be. It's been this way for as long as I can remember. I don't really know what a normal family looks like."

"They must have been in love once, though?"

He nods. "In the early days, I think they were. I've seen the photos and occasionally they reminisce about a good memory, and I see a wistful look in my mum's eyes. However, they didn't walk the same path and somewhere along the way, they split up and now walk parallel to each other. Both in the same direction, but very much on their own. Occasionally, they meet up with someone else on their respective paths who keep them company for part of the way, but ultimately, they keep on walking in sync. I'm not sure why they do, but something is keeping them connected and I like to think it's not just the company."

His words make me sad, and then he shrugs and pulls me up. "Don't feel sorry for me. As I said, it's what I'm used to. I'm just not prepared to follow their blueprint. I doubt there is that perfect life out there, anyway. Who knows, you may prove me wrong because I can't wait to meet your parents and see what living the dream is really like?"

I follow him back into the kitchen and think about my parents. They are nothing like Jack's and their home is nothing like this one. I'm ashamed that I'd been embarrassed for him to see where I come from, but now, I couldn't care less. My life is real life, not this fabricated web of lies designed to impress, which actually only repels. This house isn't comfortable. These people aren't interesting, and I can't wait to leave this magazine spread and get back to where I feel comfortable and real.

CHAPTER 16

Amanda looks up as we head back into the kitchen and says in a strained voice. "Take a seat. Dinner is almost ready. Jack, make sure you fill Nelly's glass while I summon the others."

As he heads dutifully to the fridge, I'm amazed to see Amanda pick up a silver bell lying on the island unit in the centre of the room and ring it loudly. What the…?

I daren't look at Jack and just gulp back the wine quicker than I should to stop myself from laughing.

It doesn't take long for the others to join us, and I notice that Jack's father doesn't make eye contact with Amanda. Ariadne and Godfrey take their seats and then proceed to pour over Ariadne's phone, no doubt sorting out her latest Instagram post. I feel bad for Amanda, who appears to be doing absolutely everything and say loudly, "Would you like some help, Amanda?"

She stares at me with surprise before shaking her head. "No thank you, Nelly. It's kind of you to ask, but I'm best left to my own devices. Just sit back and enjoy your meal."

She heads over and dishes out plates of spaghetti to each of us and says, "Help yourself to salad and James, make sure everyone has a drink, if it's not too much trouble."

Her voice is hard and laced with steel and I sneak a look at James, who merely smiles and says lightly, "OK, what can I get you, Nelly?"

"I'm fine thanks, Mr Mason."

He grins. "Call me James, dear. Mr Mason is so stuffy and boring."

I nod, and he turns his attention to Godfrey. "How about you, Godfrey? Do you fancy a beer?"

I giggle as Godfrey looks horrified. "No thank you, James. I'm happy with a glass of Prosecco if there's one going."

Amanda comes and takes her seat and the atmosphere is tense. She helps herself to salad and we all eat in silence. After a while, she turns to Jack and says with interest, "How's the shop going? I'm sorry we couldn't make the opening."

He shrugs and says lightly, "It's going as well as can be expected."

Ariadne wrinkles up her pert nose and says dismissively, "I can't imagine why you opened it in the first place. Aunt Alice is sure to give you your inheritance. After all, you are her favourite."

Jack appears irritated. "Shut up, Ariadne. You're talking rubbish, as usual."

She sneers. "Is that the best comeback you've got? You really are stupid, you know, Jack."

I feel a little lightheaded as Amanda bangs the table and says angrily, "Stop it, both of you. What must our guests be thinking?"

Godfrey doesn't look as if he's thinking much at all as he continues to study Ariadne's phone. James just raises his eyes and eats his food as if he's on some sort of time restriction and Amanda sighs heavily. "Slow down, James. You'll get indigestion and I'll pay for it when you can't sleep tonight."

He shrugs. "Then sleep in the guest room like you usually do."

The look she gives him would turn the milk sour, and she snaps, "If you were a gentleman, you would take the spare room from time to time. I mean, it's not too much to ask, considering you're the reason I need it."

James just throws her a warning look and I feel Jack tense beside me. Watching his family is like watching a storm break. There is so much underlying tension in the room that is simmering under the surface. Ariadne is obviously bored by it all and just examines her nails and then sighs.

"I'm never using that salon again. Look at the state of these nails. They cost me a fortune and I can see the brush strokes from here. Look, Godfrey, they're appalling."

I peer across and can't see anything wrong and she catches my eye and raises a perfectly shaped eyebrow. "Do you have Instagram, Nelly?"

I shake my head. "No."

She looks surprised. "What about Twitter?"

"No."

"Goodness, how surprising. You must be on Facebook, though."

I nod miserably. "I do have a business page on there for my shop, but I don't post much."

Ariadne and Godfrey look at me as if I have two heads and then she holds out her hand and says firmly, "Every business should have all avenues of social media. Hand me your phone and I'll set it up for you."

Jack says shortly, "Leave her alone. Knowing you, you just want to add her as another one of your followers. If Nelly wants to set up social media, she's smart enough to do it herself."

Ariadne huffs. "I'm just trying to help, Jack. You're so touchy these days. To be honest, if anyone's got a right to be touchy it's me. I'm the one about to spend the next few months in hell at the old folk's home. I'm the one who must wear some sort of–" she shivers "uniform and I'm the one who will dread going to work every day. All I can say is Aunt Alice had better follow through with her promise because if she does, I'm going to reward my sacrifice with an all-inclusive five-star trip to the Maldives with Godfrey."

Amanda says wearily. "Yes, it's going to be a tough few months, that's for sure."

Jack says slyly, "So, when's the first lesson, mum?"

Amanda visibly shivers and says dully, "Tonight, actually. That's probably why your father's home for once. We're due to start our lessons later and I'm dreading every excruciating minute of it."

James nods irritably. "Daft old bat. Fancy dreaming up this ridiculous will. Why she couldn't just leave it like everyone else does is beyond me. Mind you, she was always conniving and vindictive."

I'm shocked as Amanda says tartly, "Have some respect, James. Aunt Alice has always been good to us and if this brings her happiness, then so be it. We will just have to suck it up and do as she says and play along."

I feel ill listening to them. This isn't right. They are all monsters. How could they be so cruel? I feel a little nauseous and the food tastes like dust in my mouth. Then I feel a warm hand in mine and as Jack gently squeezes it, I feel bad for him. If this is bad for me, it's a hundred times worse for him.

Silence descends on the table, and I say tentatively, "I would love to try salsa dancing. You may really enjoy it."

James laughs loudly. "You're funny, Nelly. I think our dancing days are well and truly over. In fact, it's just an inconvenience that's getting in the way of more important things that we would rather be doing."

Amanda says derisively, "Yes, James. What is it you would rather be doing, exactly?"

I try to make myself as small as possible as they share a frosty look and Jack sighs. "Nelly's right. It may be an enjoyable experience if you give it your best shot."

Ariadne laughs shrilly, "Says the guy who came out best in all this."

Jack frowns. "For your information, mine is the most challenging."

I hold my breath as he continues. "I must run a business with staff and make it work. I have to work there all day when it's not what I want to do in life. This is Aunt Alice's dream and I'm the one living it. If I had my way, I would be backpacking around the world and far away from the madness that surrounds this family."

Ariadne wrinkles her nose again and sneers. "Good god, Jack, where's the fun in slinging on a backpack and roughing it when you can travel the world in five-star luxury?"

She laughs shrilly. "Next, you'll be telling us you want to build an orphanage in a war-torn country."

Godfrey laughs. "Could you imagine anything worse? Some guys from school did that once. I think it broke them. You should stick to your own environment and what you know best. Leave it to the people who like doing that sort of thing and spend your days enjoying life instead."

I think I hate Godfrey.

I think I hate Ariadne.

I think I hate Amanda and I have absolutely no time for James.

The trouble is, I think I love Jack because this has shown me even more why he is so special. Living among these people must be some cross to bear, and yet he isn't like them in the slightest. He is kind, considerate and funny. He hasn't complained about living Aunt Alice's dream and has gone about it with the sort of attitude that means he will succeed.

I can tell he's uncomfortable, and that makes two of us. Angela was right. You never know what's going on at home which makes people the way they are, and I'm just amazed that Jack turned out as well as he has.

CHAPTER 17

Dinner is sublime. Despite Amanda's obvious flaws, cooking is not one of them and I mean every word when I thank her for such a lovely meal. Dessert was a delicious chiffon pie that was light and melted in my mouth and the base was crunchy and delicious. The wine was obviously expensive and the surroundings impressive. However, the people sitting at that table were the worst kind. If anything, I have a new respect for Aunt Alice because it's obvious why she's done this. In fact, I'm just amazed she's leaving them anything at all and not donating it all to charity because if I were in her shoes, this family wouldn't get a penny, except for Jack, of course.

Amanda and James depart to get ready for salsa lessons, and Ariadne and Godfrey head out for drinks with friends. Jack drives me home and I can tell he's embarrassed.

"I'm sorry, Nelly, that was difficult."

"It's fine. Not every family is a textbook one. I'm guessing your family has many redeeming qualities. Maybe they just had an off night."

He shakes his head. "No, that was pretty much a normal

night at home. Maybe you should invite me to meet your parents and I can see what a proper family talks about at the dinner table."

Thinking of my family, I smile to myself. "Yes, that sounds a good idea. I'll set it up."

As we continue to drive back to my flat, I feel a sense of unease. Jack appears to have two challenges whereas the others only one. I wonder why that is?

Jack interrupts my thoughts, saying, "What are you thinking?"

"Nothing much." I hesitate and then say quickly, "One thought did cross my mind, though. Why have you got two challenges and the others only have one?"

For a moment, there's an awkward silence. It's almost as if he's playing for time because he doesn't answer right away. Then he says in a small voice. "I don't know. Maybe she thinks I need to learn the most. Perhaps I'm so far gone she wants to teach me a lesson. Who knows why, but it doesn't matter? All that does is we all carry out her wishes as requested."

Once again, I have a bitter taste in my mouth as I realise that we're tricking an old lady into believing her request is real. The silence sits heavy in the air, and I say sadly, "I can't do this."

He says sharply, "What do you mean, you can't do this?"

"Fool your aunt. It's not right and if I help you, I'm no better than your family."

He says roughly, "What are you saying?"

I falter and then say sadly. "I, I think you'll have to find someone else to help you. I'm sorry, I don't think I'm suitable for this."

To my surprise, he pulls the car over and turns to look at me with an expression that makes me hold my breath. He looks lost and vulnerable, and he reaches out and grasps my hands, saying anxiously, "Please, Nelly, don't do this. I need you; it can only be you."

I whisper, "But why? You could have anyone. Is it because you know I don't expect anything from you? I'm sure somebody like Emma would be more suitable and you have dated in the past. Who knows, if you give her another chance, you may discover you were meant to be together all along."

He grabs my hands and says urgently, "Give me one more week to convince you. I want to prove to you that you're the only one I can do this with. Please, Nelly?"

Something about the look in his eyes makes me question everything. I'm not sure why, but there's more to this than I thought.

I stare at him for a moment and then shake my head slowly. "OK, one more week. I'm not sure how you can change my mind, but I should give you the chance, at least."

I don't miss the relief in his eyes as he reaches out and impulsively pulls me close. I think my heart almost stops as he strokes my hair and murmurs, "Thank you."

Well, this is odd. I am being clasped tightly to a guy that starred in my dreams on many occasions who is grateful that I didn't just break up our fake relationship. I'm not going to lie, though; it does feel nice having someone hold me close and I suppose that's why I allow myself to relax against him and get carried away by the moment.

Maybe I should pull back and high five him or something because this feels awkward. However, I don't want to and just enjoy the moment and file it away in that memory box inside my head to call on in the future. Then he pulls back and stares into my eyes and says softly, "I don't want you going anywhere. I want to get to know you and your family, and you don't get away with that so easily."

Rolling my eyes, I try to lighten the atmosphere. "You do remember who my parents are, Jack? You won't be so keen when you're facing your old headmaster across the dinner table."

His eyes soften and he says sweetly, "Actually, I'm looking forward to it."

I almost think he's going to kiss me again, but instead, he pulls away and starts up the engine. "Come on, I'll drop you home. It's been a long day and you probably can't wait to get rid of me."

I'm slightly disappointed that he didn't kiss me and say in a high voice, "Yes, of course. Maybe we should call it a night."

* * *

Later, when I'm lying in bed reliving the evening, it crosses my mind - why me? Jack appeared so worried when I told him I was pulling out. It's only been a few days. Surely, he could find someone else.

What is so special about me?

CHAPTER 18

The next few days are routine. Working and then heading home to spend the evening alone. I see Jack at odd times during the day, mainly if he brings me a coffee, for appearance's sake, of course. Other than that, he keeps his distance.

Ken comes and says 'hi' and I'm glad to see a friendly face.

"Hey honey, how's trade?"

I try to put a brave face on. "Oh, fine. You know, things are always a little quiet this time of the year. I'm sure trade will pick up soon."

He looks concerned. "I hope you'd tell me if you were struggling? I mean, I could always give you an extension on the rent deadline."

I smile gratefully. "It's fine. I'll be ok. I've been thinking about a side venture for a while and just need time to set it up."

He says with interest. "What is it?"

"Chocolate parties. You know, provide a chocolate fountain, favours, in fact, everything you need to make your party a little different."

He smiles with approval. "That sounds like a plan. It's

always good to have ideas in business. Don't let the grass grow under your feet and all that. Anyway, I came here for a reason."

Something about the look in his eyes stops me in my tracks. He is obviously excited about something, and I say in surprise, "What is it?"

He grins, "I'm getting married."

I squeal and flinging my arms around him, say happily, "Congratulations, I can't believe it. When is the happy day?"

He laughs. "We don't want to hang around, so buy your best hat for some time next month.

"What!"

He grins. "Why wait? I've discovered a new lease of life and can't wait to make Violet my wife."

I stare at him in shock. "I'm sorry. What did you say?"

"I can't wait to make Violet my wife."

"Who's Violet?"

I stare at him in horror. "Where's Patty?"

He looks a little embarrassed and says in a small voice. "We're not together anymore."

I sit down heavily on the seat behind the counter and say in confusion, "I think you should start at the beginning."

Before he can fill me in, the door chimes and I glance up and see a glamorous woman who can't be much older than I am. She is dressed fashionably, and her make-up is perfect. Her hair is long and dark and extremely stylish, and she walks up to Ken and places her hand on his chest and purrs up at him.

"There you are, darling. I thought I'd find you in here."

I stare at them in amazement as she presses her lips to his and says flirtatiously, "How's my big, bad bear? You know, your baby bear is feeling a little hungry today."

He throws her a look I would rather not have witnessed and pulls her close and kisses her deeply, making me feel quite ill and I cough discreetly.

Ken laughs and makes the introductions. "Nelly, meet

Violet. She's been dying to meet you. I've told her everything about you."

I nod but can't quite manage a smile because it's as if she's assessing me on the spot. She smiles, but I can tell it's not genuine and she holds out a limp hand and says, "I'm pleased to meet you, Nelly."

I have so many questions that need answers, but Ken just pulls her tightly against him and says in a gruff voice. "We had better be off. I promised Violet I'd treat her to lunch in that posh place in town. See you later."

I watch in horror as they head outside and wonder what sort of parallel universe I am now living in, where everything is topsy-turvy and not what it seems anymore. First Jack and now Ken. Whatever is next?

CHAPTER 19

Luckily, life returns to normality for a few days, and I concentrate on my business. I wasn't lying when I mentioned to Ken I was branching out and spend some time investigating what running parties would involve. Since Jack opened opposite, it's made me realise that I need to up my game, and I started studying my business with a fresh pair of eyes.

Angela pops by on the odd occasion, but other than her, I haven't seen anyone. Business is steady but not brilliant and I wonder how much longer I can exist without any real customers, rather than the ones who just stop by for a chat.

However, tonight will be interesting because Jack's coming home with me to meet my parents and the thought is making me feel quite ill. I wonder what they will make of all this.

* * *

THIS TIME I drive and am a little ashamed as Jack sits beside me in my beat-up old Beetle. I've always considered it quirky and fun, but after the elegance of Jack's car, it just seems dated and scruffy. I'm not the tidiest person in the world and am embarrassed when I spy the crumbs on the floor and the crisp wrappers in the door compartments. Jack, however, doesn't appear to notice and just smiles at me reassuringly while I grate the gears nervously as we head to my parent's house.

After a while, he says with interest, "So, what does your mother do?"

"She's a teacher. She works at Vincent Primary school and teaches year six."

"Why didn't you become a teacher?"

I make a face. "You must be joking. I hated school for obvious reasons and couldn't wait to leave. I suppose to outsiders I must be a disappointment to my family. My parents are in a respected profession and my sister is at Oxford, following in their academic footsteps."

He says with surprise, "But you were always clever at school."

I shrug dismissively. "So what? Just because you do well in academic things doesn't mean you have to carry it on. As I said, I always wanted my own shop, and I didn't need any qualifications for that. Just a lot of hard work and good intentions. Who knows, maybe I'll have a chain of them and be international before I'm thirty. Success is measured in different ways, Jack, and some may argue that I'm actually the more successful one in my family. They would be wrong, but I like to believe I stand a small chance of gaining that title one day."

He laughs, which makes my heart flutter. Jack's laugh is as sexy as he is and it's quite distracting when I'm trying to drive. In fact, all I want to do is openly stare at him because the sight of Jack Mason in my car is one I never thought I'd see in a million years.

* * *

We pull out outside a modest home in a respectable suburb and, unlike Jack's parent's house, mine is a little shabby and in need of a sixty-minute makeover. The garden is laid mainly to lawn because my parents don't have time for gardening and would never think of employing a gardener. The interior probably hasn't changed from my youth because why change something that isn't broken? Everything in this house serves a purpose and any designer touches are sorely lacking. Even the wallpaper is from the seventies, which is a good thing because it's come full circle and is now fashionable due to the current seventies retro revival going on.

It's never bothered me in the past, but now as I see it through Jack's eyes, I'm ashamed to admit that I'm embarrassed by my parent's home.

However, I'm not ashamed of my parents and as my mum opens the door, I smile at the woman I love more than any other.

Bettina Gray is a practically dressed, no-nonsense type of woman who is polite in company and a riot in private. A typical teacher in her knee-length tweed skirt, sensible blouse, and tank top. I don't think I've ever seen makeup on her face and her hairstyle hasn't changed since the day I was born. She wears glasses and comfortable shoes and is in direct contrast to the chic elegance of Amanda. However, the smile in her eyes matches the one on her face, and she appears genuinely delighted to see us.

She shakes Jack's hand warmly and says softly, "I'm pleased to meet you, Jack. Nelly has told us so much about you." My cheeks flame as I try to brush off her comment, because Jack doesn't need to know that I've boasted constantly about my amazing new boyfriend. The trouble is, I have never had one to boast about before and so I've gone a little overboard on my descriptions to my family.

Jack smiles politely, but I don't miss the smirk in his eyes.

Can eyes smirk? Looking at the expression in his I can assure you they can and I can't even look at him as I follow my mum inside.

As we reach the crowded living room, my dad stands and comes forward, beaming broadly. "Jack Mason. I remember you. You were one of our shining football stars. It's good to see you again."

I almost want to place my hands over my eyes and peek through my fingers because I'm dreading how Jack must be feeling right now. However, he stands a little straighter and says politely, "It's good to see you again, sir."

My father laughs. "You can drop the sir. Mr Gray will do fine."

Jack laughs nervously as dad winks and says loudly, "Just joking, son. Call me Tom."

Jack now looks quite ill as he says nervously, "Thank you… um… Tom."

Dad nods towards the settee. "Take a seat, Jack. I'm sure Nelly won't mind helping her mother with some refreshments while we get reacquainted with one another."

I almost bolt from the room, happy to leave this awkward situation behind me. As far as I'm concerned, Jack's on his own because he made this mess and now he's going to have to deal with the consequences.

As I help my mum make some tea, she says softly, "Jack seems nice, Nelly."

I smile and try to ignore the prickle of guilt inside me as I realise we are lying to my family as much as Aunt Alice. This doesn't seem right, and I feel uneasy.

So, I just nod. "Its early days and we're more like um… good friends, really."

Then, to my surprise, my mum winks suggestively and giggles. "With benefits, I hope."

I stare at her in shock as she grins in amusement. "You

should see your face, Nelly. You forget that I was once a young girl myself. I haven't always been so respectable, you know."

Words fail me as I try to drive away the images springing to mind about my mother being anything less than one hundred per cent respectable. However, she just sighs and says wistfully, "You know, I was a little wild in my youth. There was this time I was caught kissing a boy from my class in the corridor. My parents were called in and I was suspended for a day."

I stare at her in disbelief. "You're kidding."

She giggles. "No. I'm not. You know, we're all the same in our youth. I was the wild one in my family and thought nothing of sneaking a few mouthfuls from my parent's drinks cabinet before heading out to meet the local bad boy."

I wonder if it would be rude to put my hands over my ears because I absolutely do not want to hear this.

She sighs again. "Luke Carpenter was his name. I've never forgotten him. All leather jackets and bad intentions. I've never felt as alive as I did in his arms. He awoke the woman in me, and it was touch and go whether I would even finish school. Those were heady times, and I lost my mind as well as my heart."

As I stare at her, I'm mesmerised. She has a lost expression on her face that reaches out to me. A yearning for the past and what might have been, and I say softly, "Did you love him… this Luke Carpenter?"

She leans against the sink and nods dreamily. "He was my first love. I adored him, but he was bad, Nelly. He used to fight – a lot. He rode a motorbike and never once wore a helmet. He kept me out late at night and introduced me to everything a respectable girl should never know. I have never forgotten him and hope I never will."

Edging closer, I whisper, "What happened?"

She lowers her voice. "He went to prison. Got arrested for

breaking into a local councillor's house. He stole some things, and they threw away the key."

I stare at her in shock because the girl she is describing is the polar opposite of the mother I know and love.

I say incredulously, "What did Nan and Grandad say?"

She shrugs. "What didn't they say, more like. I was transferred to an all-girl's school, and they watched me like a hawk. My evenings were spent with various tutors, and I was made to join every club and society going to occupy my evil mind. As you know, I grew up and became the respectable adult they wanted me to be, and then I met your father."

Shaking my head, I picture my father compared to the local bad boy Luke Carpenter and feel a little disappointed for my mother, although I know I shouldn't.

She smiles mysteriously. "Don't always believe in outward impressions, Nelly. Your father more than measured up to Luke Carpenter; you don't have to worry about that."

I am now trying desperately to shake the mental image I have of my father morphing into the local bad boy behind closed doors and giggle. "Are you saying dad was a little wild in his youth?"

Mum winks. "I'm saying nothing of the kind. Now, hadn't we better head inside to rescue your new boyfriend from the third degree?"

It's as if I'm having an out-of-body experience as I follow her into the living room, carrying the tray of tea things. The first thing I hear as we head into the room is my dad saying, "So, just what are your intentions towards my daughter?"

I almost drop the tray when I register Jack's terrified expression while my father sits opposite him, looking stern and forbidding.

Mum laughs and says gently, "Stop scaring Jack, Tom."

She turns to Jack and smiles sweetly. "Don't pay any attention to my husband, Jack. He forgets sometimes that he's not at work."

She hands Jack a cup of tea in the usual bone china teacup they reserve for guests and special occasions, and winks. "Would you like a custard cream with that?"

He smiles politely. "Yes please, Mrs Gray."

Shaking her head, she piles a few on a plate and says warmly, "Call me Betty."

Jack smiles as I roll my eyes.

After a while, the conversation turns to Jack's family and when my parents hear that Amanda and James are taking salsa lessons, things deteriorate quickly. I watch in surprise as they share a look between them, and my mother says excitedly, "Salsa. Oh, how amazing."

She grins. "Tom, do you remember how to do it?"

He nods and then, to my horror, they jump up and start bumping and grinding suggestively in front of our eyes. I can't even look at Jack as my parents appear to lose themselves in the moment and start acting out some sort of X-rated scene from Dirty Dancing and I am utterly mortified. Then things get even worse when my mum grabs Jack's hand and says, "Dance with me, Jack."

My father grabs mine and every nerve ending inside me screams to make this go away. Dad laughs as he holds me in his arms and propels me like a stiff board around the room, while I try not to notice that my mother is pressed against Jack, who is completely out of his comfort zone.

I'm pretty sure if he knew this was how the evening would pan out, he wouldn't have been quite so keen to come.

After the most horrible five minutes of my life, they take pity on us and release us back to the safety of the couch, and my mum laughs happily. "I forgot how much fun salsa is. Where do your parents go for their lessons, Jack? Maybe we should start again, Tom. It would spice things up a little."

WHEN CUPID MISSED

Jack almost bursts out laughing at my expression as I implore him with my eyes and a slight shake to my head not to tell them, but he responds by saying, "They go to the Armitage Centre in town. I think the lessons are on a Tuesday and Thursday."

Mum claps her hand and yells, "Surf the net and see if we can join Tom. It would be such fun."

She says with excitement, "Why don't you join us? It would be wonderful if we could all share something in common."

Shaking my head firmly, I say quickly, "I'm sorry, but we don't have time for it. We are both running businesses that don't stop demanding our time when the doors close at night. Maybe when we're both successful, we will think again, but now is not that time."

My mother laughs. "You are so serious, Nelly. You always were such a funny little thing. You know Jack, Nelly has always been a little strange. There was this one time when she was about seven, she had these little knickers with the days of the week printed on each of them. She always insisted on wearing the correct pair that corresponded with the day and went into a meltdown when she couldn't find her 'Tuesday' knickers."

I stare at her in horror – she is really going there with this and I can't believe what I'm hearing.

She peers across at my father and giggles. "Do you remember, Tom? The cat brought them in one day from the garden. Apparently, she had wet herself and buried them there rather than admit it. Oh, how we laughed about that."

The blood drains from my face as Jack raises his eyes and tries not to laugh. My parents, however, laugh fit to burst and then my father says loudly, "What about when she had that crush on some boy from school. What was his name again?"

I jump up and say tightly, "Enough of the trip down memory lane. We've got to leave, immediately, in fact. I'm sorry, but you know how it is with us, um, business owners. No time for frivolity and lots to do and all that. Thanks for the tea, but we really must be going."

I reach out and pull Jack's arm almost out of its socket as I march with determination towards the door, vowing to maintain a huge distance between us all from now on. How embarrassing. I can't believe my father would even remember that. The fact the boy in question was sitting right there makes everything a million times worse.

My parents follow me to the door and my father says, "Good to see you again, Mason. Remember, I've got my eye on you. Respect my daughter and you'll be fine."

My mother laughs, "Enough Tom. Drop the overprotective father act before I tell Jack exactly what we got up to behind our parent's backs."

Out of the corner of my eye, I see his hand snake around her waist and then move up to cup her breast, as he nips her neck sharply with his teeth. I can tell that Jack notices because he is struggling to stop laughing and I feel my cheeks flaming as red as my decrepit car waiting to transport us back to normality.

Shouting, "Bye", I drag Jack away, vowing never to return – with any of the male species ever again.

Their parting shot chills me to the bone as my mother cries out, "We'll introduce ourselves to your parents at salsa, Jack. It will be good to get to know them."

I almost push Jack into the passenger seat before proving that old beetles really can do 0-60 at the speed of light.

As evenings go, that was the worst one of my life.

CHAPTER 20

Jack is still laughing when I pull up outside his apartment block and I say apologetically, "I'm so sorry about my parents. You have every right to think I had a bad childhood, but let me tell you nothing compares to what I've just experienced. It can only be described as child abuse. Parents should be issued with a government health warning - approach with caution. All your secrets and worse fears may be realised."

Jack laughs. "I liked them. At least they like each other. I would spend every evening with your parents rather than mine. I hope I'm as happy as they are after so many years together."

I stare at him in total disbelief. "You're a strange guy, Jack."

"Why?"

"Because of all this. You open a shop selling things no ordinary boy would be interested in. Then you ask a girl to be your partner in crime who you never looked at twice in the past when there are so many more suitable ones surrounding you every day. Then you spend time with the pre-mentioned girl, visiting her parents, who quite honestly should have been certified years ago and yet somehow you appear to be enjoying yourself."

He stares at me with a strange expression and says softly, "You've met my family. It's not quite the dream you thought it was. As for ignoring you at school, well, I'm guilty of that, I suppose. However, you never spoke to me either."

I'm taken by surprise, and it makes me think back on those years. It's true, I never once spoke to him. I suppose I was too busy feigning disinterest in somebody I knew I never stood a chance with. In private, however, my fantasies were off the scale where it concerned him, and I'm sure I wasn't the only one. Jack Mason was that guy in school. You know, the one every girl wanted and only a few privileged girls got to experience. Yes, his name decorated various notebooks of mine, surrounded by hearts and our initials, and I'm probably not alone there.

I say with interest, "What about you? What was it really like being you at school? Did you feel the pressure of being the popular guy in class or didn't you realise you were?"

The expression in Jack's eyes holds my attention for a split second longer than it should have . He gazes at me so intently I forget to breathe as he says lightly, "I never thought about it, I suppose. I was only interested in football and messing around with my mates. Of course, I was interested in the girls who surrounded me. It was easy."

To my surprise, he reaches out and takes my hand in his and says softly, "But where's the fun in that, Nelly? Surely the real interest lies in the challenge. The one you can't have and the one just out of reach. That's the one who holds your attention and makes you think of when you're alone. They are the one thing you can't have, and you spend hours thinking of ways to get the prize. I'm competitive and always have been. I want what's just out of reach. I always have. Once it's mine, I lose interest and I'm onto the next challenge. That's why I'll never settle down because I haven't yet met the equal of me. Someone who pushes me to be better. I'm everything you thought I was and worse. Girls don't deserve men like me in their life because I am the selfish boy from school that you remember. Girls like you meet the men nature intended them to meet and leave the drama to girls like Emma who thrive on it."

Snatching my hand away, I stare at him with a cold expression. "You're every bit as much of an arsehole as I thought you were back then. I can see you've learned nothing since leaving school, and it will make my job here a lot easier. Take the money and run, that's what I'll do because the sooner you and your chocolate pretending shop leave town, the better off we'll all be."

My heart beats as furiously as I am as I stare at the person before me. Then I say angrily, "You know, Jack, you may be everything to all women on the outside, but inside you're as empty as an Easter egg these days. Enticing on the outside, promising much when you unwrap the packaging, only to leave the bitter taste of disappointment inside when you open it and realise there's nothing but air in there. Maybe you should be on your own because the poor girl that ends up with you would have a miserable life. Now, you had better leave because I have a business to run and need my beauty sleep."

To my extreme annoyance, Jack just laughs and smiles, flicking me that annoying 'ok I'll forgive you everything' look.

"Now I've upset you and I didn't mean to. I am grateful to you for helping me out, but you need to realise something about me. I'm not the happy ever after. I'm not Prince Charming and I'm not 'The One.' As soon as I can, I'll be packing my bags and heading off on a plane quicker than you can blink. I'm every bit as selfish as my parents because they created me in their image. However, that doesn't mean we can't enjoy this relationship while we have it. Let's just have some fun and treat it for what it is."

Taking deep, calming breaths and trying desperately to find some freaking zen in my life, I say in a low voice laced with the controlled rage of a serial killer, "Get out."

Jack shakes his head and smirks. "It's ok, I'm leaving. I'll see you tomorrow, babe."

The door slams behind him and I waste no time in tearing up the tarmac and getting as far away from him as possible.

What just happened? It was all going so well and then he changed in seconds. Nice Jack became cocky Jack in the blink of an eye, and it's made my mission much easier. I will help him just to get rid of him and if he thinks it will be fun, he's got another thing coming.

CHAPTER 21

I'm still seething when I open Chocolatti the next morning, and I'm determined I won't even look across the street today. In fact, I even consider taking down the spy mirror and pretending Jack and his stupid shop don't exist.

I'm still fuming around mid-morning when the door chimes and I glance up to see Patty heading inside looking dreadful.

She peers around her nervously and I register the huge dark circles under her eyes and the pale complexion of a woman who looks as if she's had no sleep.

I say with a hint of concern, "Patty. It's lovely to see you."

She scurries over and glances around her furtively. "Hi, Nelly. Um… I'm sorry, but is Ken around?"

I shake my head. "No, I'm sorry. I haven't seen him today."

She sighs with relief. "Good."

"What happened? Ken came in here and told me he was marrying another woman."

The expression of pain and surprise in her eyes takes my breath away as she says shakily, "Married?"

Then her shoulders sag and a lone tear trickles down her

cheek. I can't bear it and head towards her and wrap my arm around her, saying gently, "Are you ok?"

Sniffing, she says in a whisper, "No, I don't think I am."

Pulling her into the little room behind the counter, I offer her a seat and flick on the kettle. "Tell me what happened. Maybe we can make some sense of it between us."

She sniffs loudly and then blows her nose into a tissue. "It's terrible, Nelly. I don't know what happened, but it all started when my sister came to stay. I know Ken doesn't like her and told me all the time she was staying, he would stay away. To be honest, I wish I could have done the same, but when I hadn't heard from him for a couple of days, I got worried. I tried to call, but it just went to voicemail. I thought he'd had an accident and tried frantically to reach him. Then, a couple of days ago, I got a text from him saying he no longer wanted to be with me, and we should call it quits."

She starts to sob, and I stare at her in shock. "A text!"

She nods. "It was so cold. I tried to call, but I still couldn't get through. Then yesterday he called. At least I thought it was him."

She sniffs and says in a broken voice. "It was a woman. She sounded so cold and told me that Ken didn't want to talk to me and had moved on already. I wasn't to contact him and if I knew what was good for me, I would stay away."

"She threatened you!"

"Yes, it felt like that."

I stare at her in disbelief. "That's terrible, Patty. It doesn't make sense. I mean, I've met this woman. I think her name's Violet. They came in here yesterday and I'm not joking. There's something strange about all this. You know, I disliked her on the spot, and I think she's controlling Ken. Maybe she's a witch or some sort of high priestess in a cult. Yes, that's the most likely explanation."

Patty almost laughs. "You're mad, Nelly."

Shrugging, I hand her a cup of strong tea and say angrily, "Well, I'll find out what's going on. No young, attractive woman is going to get in the way of the couple I love who were meant to be together. I'm making it my mission to destroy that cosy bubble she's trapped him in; you just watch me."

Patty smiles miserably through her tears. "You're such a good friend, Nelly."

Handing her a little taster chocolate for her nerves, I cram a few into my mouth to help me chew on the problem. Yes, Violet is playing with fire and is about to get burned.

Later that afternoon, Jack sidles into the shop sheepishly, holding a latte and says apologetically, "Peace offering."

Fixing him with a withering stare, I say angrily, "If you think a latte will excuse your outburst yesterday, you're more deluded than I thought."

He sets the cup down and says in a worried voice, "Listen, I didn't mean to come across so cold last night. I suppose it was the visit to your parents that set me off. When I saw how happy they were, it made me think about my own. Maybe they loved each other once, but it's now pretty obvious that love turned to hate. I saw my future mapped out before me, where I will be no better than them. You deserve so much better, and I felt bad for involving you in my plan. Let me make it up to you tonight. We could catch a movie or something, and just try to enjoy ourselves for once."

I say with exasperation. "That's what I don't understand. It's fine for us to pretend to be a couple when the situation warrants it, but from what I can see, we've only needed to do it twice. Why the cosy evenings alone? What purpose do they solve?"

"We need to get to know one another. Be familiar in company and have a connection. Aunt Alice is shrewd and will notice if we don't feel comfortable with each other. The trouble is, we don't have long, which is why I braved coming over here."

"What do you mean?"

He sighs heavily. "We've all been asked to dinner on Sunday. The whole family, that is. She wants to meet up and see how we're coping. Obviously, as my girlfriend, you're invited, and it would be good for you to meet her and see what we're facing for yourself."

Suddenly, I'm feeling more nervous than I felt sitting my final exams and say faintly, "We're doomed. She'll see through this charade immediately. I'm not sure if I can do this."

Jack smiles reassuringly and says with more confidence than I feel, "You'll be fine. No, we'll be fine. It's only dinner and the rest of the family will be there. I have every confidence in you."

We are interrupted by Emma, who pops her head around the door and says anxiously, "I'm sorry, Jack, but the local walking club has just arrived and its cream teas all round. We need you back."

She smirks at me as Jack rolls his eyes. "No peace for the wicked."

Then to answer every prayer I ever offered to the love gods, he reaches across and pulls my face to his, saying sexily, "Duty calls, babe. I'll see you after work."

Then he kisses me with a long, lingering, soul-scorching, panty melting kiss that sends Emma into one of her petulant moods and me into a state of euphoria, causing me to instantly forgive him.

CHAPTER 22

Sunday arrives like a bad dose of the flu. My knees start shaking, and I get palpitations before I even decide what to wear. To say I'm dreading this is an understatement. A whole day with Jack's annoying family. Why on earth did I agree to this?

It turns out that Aunt Alice lives in the Cotswolds, which involves a two-hour car journey. I was hoping we would be driving there ourselves and heart sank when Jack explained that we would be travelling in his father's Range Rover. The only consolation is that I get to sit squashed up next to Jack, while Godfrey is banished to the seat in the back because Ariadne doesn't want him creasing her new top.

Amanda and James look like a couple from a magazine. He is smartly dressed in chinos and a polo shirt, and his aftershave is seriously overpowering. Amanda is dressed in a smart shift dress, with elegant jewellery tying the look together, and her makeup and hair are immaculate.

Ariadne is no different and looks as if she's stepped from the pages of a catalogue and Godfrey looks as idiotic as usual with checked trousers and a blazer, over which is tied the proverbial pink Ralph Lauren jumper. His sunglasses are sweeping his floppy hair back from his face and his attention is firmly glued to his phone.

Jack looks mouth-watering in smart black jeans and a polo shirt, with his hair slightly spiky on top. He smells so amazing, I have an overpowering urge to spend the whole journey sniffing him but decide against it because I'm trying to play it cool.

I, on the other hand, look as respectable as my budget will allow. The local bargain shop is a find for designer labels from seasons past and I'm wearing a tailored skirt with a smart off the shoulder top and stilettos. I resemble a secretary, but that can't be helped; it was this or my scruffy jeans.

Almost before we've left the end of the drive, they are annoying me. James starts the engine and Amanda snaps, "Oh, for goodness' sake, James, you've left the bathroom window open. How many more times must I brief you on security in the home?"

He snaps, "I don't live alone, Amanda. You spend so long in there I thought it was classed as your room."

He slams the door irritably as he heads back into the house and Amanda grumbles. "Every time. For a man who runs a company, he certainly has no common sense."

Nobody says anything and I resort to biting my fingernails, feeling awkward. James soon returns and, without a word, starts the engine and reverses at speed onto the road. He cuts the corner and Amanda screeches. "Mind the flowers. Honestly, James, you've got a rear-view camera in this car. Why do you insist on not looking at it?"

He shouts, "Do you want to drive because it feels like it?"

"I may as well because at this rate, we'll never get there."

"Just shut up, Amanda, and leave me in peace. Your constant back seat driving drives me around the bend. Listen to some music or go to sleep because you are seriously annoying me."

Luckily, Ariadne changes the subject and groans. "Dad, stop. I forgot my headphones. I can't survive hours in this car listening to Radio two. You'll have to go back."

James explodes. "For God's sake, Ariadne, you spent long enough getting ready. I asked everyone if they had everything."

She shrieks, "I can't think of everything with you pacing up and down the hallway and shouting 'are you ready yet?' You've only got yourself to blame, you know."

Amanda shouts, "James, just drive back and stop complaining. We haven't even got to the end of the road yet. I can't put up with one of her moods, today of all days."

James swears like a trooper, and I wish I'd thought of purchasing some noise reduction headphones because this is awful.

We watch Ariadne stomp inside and it's a good five minutes before she comes back in a leisurely fashion. James shouts, "Get a move on! We haven't got all day!"

She rolls her eyes and makes a big show of plugging in her headphones while totally ignoring him. Godfrey then pipes up, "As we're here, I don't suppose I could use the toilet?"

Amanda shakes her head and says in a tight voice, "James, open the door and let Godfrey use the facilities."

As James throws Godfrey a murderous look, she says angrily, "If anyone else needs to use the bathroom, please do so now."

Ariadne takes her chance to head inside and Amanda sighs irritably. "Every single bloody time. This family can't leave like a normal one. It's no wonder I drink."

Jack sighs irritably, and she says, "Don't you start, Jack. You can keep your moods to yourself today."

He shouts, "What have I done?"

She shakes her head. "You're just like your father. He has that irritable sigh syndrome as well. No words spoken, just that annoying sigh of disapproval. Well, let me tell you now, nobody likes a sighing man, it's most, well… unmanly."

Jack stares at me in disbelief and I try to disguise a fit of the giggles that are best held in because this situation is tense enough already.

Luckily, the others return and James shouts, "Right, that's it, no more returning for anything."

Ariadne suddenly yells, "I didn't check my straighteners! They could still be on."

Suddenly, the words that spill from James's lips educate me in a whole new vocabulary of swear words as Ariadne heads back inside once again to check on her electrical situation. It must be twenty minutes after we first left that we finally turn the corner at the end of the road.

However, that doesn't stop Amanda. "James, why did you turn left there? You know the quickest way to the motorway is along Green lane."

Punching the steering wheel, James yells, "Don't tell me which way to go. Green lane is on a diversion in case you've forgotten."

She nods. "Oh yes, it was most annoying when I was late for Pilates at the country club."

As we speed along, she says loudly, "Look, the Bensons have a Tesla. I think that's very green of them. Maybe we should invest in one, James?"

Shaking his head, James snarls, "If you think I'm spending a small mortgage on a car that needs to be plugged into the national grid, you're very much mistaken. I'm pretty sure it's a false economy, anyway."

Jack says with interest. "Not in the long run. I'm pretty sure we'll all be electric in the next twenty years."

James snarls, "Then let the bloody government foot the bill if they want us forking out thousands for green energy. They make it impossible to afford and tax the rest of us in punishment because we can't."

Amanda snorts, "Says the man driving a petrol guzzling Range Rover. You're such a hypocrite, James. Your carbon footprint must be through the roof. You know, you really should be more ecologically aware."

In response, James turns up the radio, effectively drowning Amanda out. Angrily, she turns it down and says icily, "Keep your tantrums to yourself, darling. You know it doesn't agree with your digestive system."

Ariadne nods her head along to her music beside me as she scrolls through her phone. She sees me looking and pulls out her earbuds and says happily, "Look at this, Nelly. I have three thousand Instagram followers as of yesterday."

She holds up her phone and I see her pouting image staring out at me wearing a bikini. She says excitedly, "I got five hundred likes on this one inside thirty minutes. You know, at this rate, I'll be an Instagram influencer before you know it."

As she scrolls through, something catches my eye and I stare at it in shock. She notices my expression and laughs shrilly. "Amazing, isn't it?"

I say faintly, "Um… who is that?"

She giggles. "Myrtle Everidge. She's one of the residents at Sunnydays care home. You know, I was absolutely dreading this job, but it's actually really fab. The residents are so amazing and the photos I've taken have been pure gold."

She thrusts the phone in my face, and I see her pouting beside a wrinkled old lady who is wearing bright pink lipstick and appears to have false eyelashes on. The caption reads, 'You're never too old to look fabulous.'

She giggles and scrolls through some more, each more disturbing than the last. Endless pictures of the residents posing beside or behind her, all either dressed like Kim Kardashian or Kanye.

Ariadne grins. "They are so much fun. I've been educating

them in social media, and we've been having a ball. Some of them even have phones, so I've set them up with their own Instagram feeds. You know, I am taking my job seriously to enlighten them about the digital age. They are having so much fun with it and I must say it's a full-time job. Mrs Benson told me I was like a breath of fresh air to the place, and I've even set up the Sunnydays blog. The resident's families are encouraged to follow it to see how their relatives are doing. I've even set up guest spots where I interview the residents and give them a makeover. I'm now responsible for the entertainment schedule and have already booked the local Little Mix tribute act a week next Thursday. You should come. It will be amazing."

Jack snorts beside me. "Trust you, Ariadne. I'm not sure this is what Aunt Alice had in mind when she set you this challenge."

Shrugging, she plugs in her earbuds and says smugly, "Just making the most of a bad situation. To be honest, I'm quite enjoying myself."

By now we've reached the motorway and James shouts, "Bloody M25! Look, the traffic's only going about 10mph. It will be Monday before we get there."

Amanda sighs. "It will soon start moving. Just stay in the same lane and we'll get there."

James shouts, "Stop telling me how to drive!"

He starts dodging the traffic by changing lanes and every time he slams on the brakes we fall forward to many loud, angry horns behind us.

Amanda yells, "James, I told you to stay in the same lane. You won't get there any faster. That lorry was behind us a minute ago, and now it's five in front."

James tightens his lips and starts banging the steering wheel. "Whose idea was this, anyway? The last thing I want to do is spend my Sunday on the M25."

Jack groans. "Same here."

Amanda says angrily, "Stop moaning. You know why we're going. Anyway, there's a service station ahead. We can stop and grab a coffee to go and some flowers for Aunt Alice."

James yells. "We've only just left home! Why do you want to stop now?"

Amanda says slightly guiltily, "Because we need petrol, anyway."

The silence is tense as we wait for James to blow his very short fuse and he says in a calm, controlled voice, laced with steel, "Why didn't you tell me this before?"

Amanda sighs. "You've got eyes, haven't you? Why didn't you notice when you started the engine? Goodness, James, must I think of everything?"

I think I'm losing the will to live as James pulls the car angrily across three lanes to reach the slip road to the service station. Nobody dares speak as he screeches into a space and says tightly, "Go and get your coffees, magazines, sweets, take a natural break and do what the bloody hell you want to because this is the freaking last time I'm stopping until we get there."

Like a pit stop in formula one, we all hurry inside the services, grateful for some fresh air. By the time we get to the car and then fill up with petrol, we have only gone a few miles in one hour. As James starts the car to pull back onto the motorway, Godfrey shouts, "Are we there yet?"

Five voices shout back angrily, "Shut up, Godfrey!"

CHAPTER 23

One hour and thirty minutes later, after the most excruciating journey, we pull up outside a house that I can only describe as belonging in Midsomer Murders. Crumbling bricks are decorated with trailing ivy holding them together and a garden that was once great, wraps around the property. There is no sound other than birds singing beautifully in the old oak trees that dominate a garden that has seen better days. Briefly, I wonder why Aunt Alice doesn't spend her money on herself because this house needs a complete overhaul.

We pile out of the car and I'm grateful to stretch my legs because even though there was a lot of room in the back of the car, it's as if I was born there due to the interminable length of that journey.

I watch with amusement as Ariadne takes a selfie of herself and Godfrey and hashtags the life out of the picture for Instagram. #familydaysout #mylove #familymatters #lovemyman #memories are now plastered over cyberspace reminding the rest of the world what life's all about.

James and Amanda lead us forward and knock on the large wooden door that hides under a crumbling porch.

However, the lady who answers the door is nothing like I imagined. Standing before us, beaming happily, is possibly the healthiest pensioner I have ever met.

Aunt Alice is tall and willowy and appears to be dressed in fitness gear. She is wearing lycra leggings with an oversized sweatshirt and her grey hair is held back by an Alice band. Her eyes shine with excitement, and I find myself smiling with genuine warmth as she beams around at us all. "Welcome, come in, come in. Don't stand on ceremony."

She ushers us inside, and I gaze around with interest. Bare wooden floors, hold in place antique furniture that was probably once considered chic and designer. Now, however, it could use a good coat of Annie Sloan paint to bring it up to speed with the modern world. Dark panelling creates a gloomy entrance, and the rest of the house isn't much better.

As we follow her into her living room, I can smell the mustiness that comes with age as I take in the large tapestries on the walls and the silver polished candlesticks and photo frames set around the room. The settee is woven with intricate bird and flower designs and appears to hold all the dust of the past in its cushions. I wish I'd taken an antihistamine because this much dust is sure to bring on my allergies.

There are none of the modern conveniences we take for granted here. Old wall lights hug the walls, looking as if they are on their last legs, cowering under their yellowing shades with fringing around them. The ancient television that sits on a side table peers at us apologetically from the corner of the room and I wonder if it's even a colour one. French doors lead to an impressive garden that went to seed years ago and crumbling walls hold the lawn back from the stone patio that has weeds growing up between the slabs.

Ariadne wrinkles up her nose and briefly dusts a cushion off before perching on the edge of the sofa. Amanda glances at Aunt Alice and smiles.

"Let me help you with the refreshments."

Aunt Alice waves her away and looks across at me and smiles. "You must be Nelly. Jack told me you would be here. Let me look at you."

I sense the attention shift in the room onto me and feel like shrivelling up in a ball of embarrassment as I stand quivering under her razor-sharp stare.

"Lovely my dear. Why don't you come and help me bring in the tea things?"

Nodding, I bypass an irritated Amanda and follow Aunt Alice towards a kitchen that should be in a museum. Formica must have been the height of luxury once, because this kitchen is fashioned entirely from it. However, I instantly fall in love with Aunt Alice because as soon as we get inside the room, she closes the door and rolls her eyes. "There, that should keep the nutters out."

As I stare at her in surprise, she giggles adorably. "They may be my family, Nelly, but they are an acquired taste. You seem fairly normal, so I thought I'd rescue you for a bit. That journey must have driven you to drink."

I wonder if this is a test and murmur, "No, it was fine. Thank you for inviting me. You are very kind."

She waves my comment away and her eyes flash mischievously. "It's ok, dear, you can drop the act. I know my family and they're the reason I hide out here in the sticks. Amanda may be my sister's daughter, God rest her soul, but she's always been a spoilt bitch and as for that idiot she married, well, let's just say she could have done better. It's no wonder their children turned out the way they did, although…" She winks and grins. "I do have high hopes for them. Maybe it's not too late and they will redeem themselves. I'm certainly hoping, anyway."

She starts to gather the drinks onto a tray, and I say politely. "You have a lovely home."

Laughing, she fixes me with the expression of a woman who can smell a lie from another county. "It's a hovel, darling. To be honest, I try not to come home much at all. Most of the time, I live in Miami in a modern apartment by the sea. Much more my thing, but occasionally I must return home to settle my affairs as they say."

I say with interest. "You live in Miami. That's amazing."

She nods. "It is. When my husband died, I couldn't get on the plane fast enough. I've always loved it there. So alive and vibrant and full of interesting people. To be honest, I want to live there full time but circumstances dictate I should spend some time here. So, I suffer my punishment and just use the time to catch up with old friends and indulge my hobbies when I do."

I acknowledge her clothing. "So, you work out then."

She nods enthusiastically. "Yes, every day. My favourite is body pump, but I also recognise the need for yoga and the odd session of spinning."

Picturing Aunt Alice in a spinning class brings a smile to my lips, and she laughs. "Not quite the image you had of me, I'm guessing."

"Not really, but then again, it's a pleasant surprise."

She fixes me with a shrewd look and says with interest. "Jack tells me you have a shop. I want to hear all about it because I'm not sure if he told you, but that's always been a dream of mine."

I say curiously, "Why didn't you open one?"

She shrugs. "I followed my husband around the world with his job. In my youth, women were expected to do that. There was none of the independence your generation takes for granted. It didn't matter because I loved my life, anyway. My husband was very successful and provided us with a comfortable life. We went to many exotic places and opening a shop would have been an inconvenience. However, you must be living the dream because I understand you sell chocolate."

Reaching into my bag, I draw out a little box that I gift wrapped for her and say, "I brought you some to try. These are my favourites, so I hope you like them. Chocolate pralines with a truffle centre."

Her eyes gleam as she takes the box from my shaking hands and smiles with genuine delight. "Thank you, my dear. I really appreciate the gesture. So, tell me about Jack. How long have you been dating?"

I feel the nerves shaking me inside as I say lightly, "Only a few weeks. We met when he opened in direct competition to me, and I recognised him from school."

She laughs and says with a gleam in her eye, "Direct competition. That's tough."

I feel the anger return and say icily, "I can tell you, Aunt Alice, I was not impressed. I told him in no uncertain terms that he should remove every trace of chocolate from his shop, but he wouldn't. Can you believe that? Opening opposite an established business and selling the same product. Business suicide, if you ask me."

She says in a thoughtful voice, "For which business, though?"

I nod gloomily. "If I were a betting woman, which I'm not, I would say mine because Jack is the local girl magnet and they flock to his shop, just grateful for the excuse to hang out in his presence."

She throws me a keen look. "So, why did you go out with him? Was it that, keep your enemy's close, kind of thing?"

Lowering my voice, I whisper, "The thing is, what you don't know is I went to school with Jack. I was in his class, and he never once spoke to me. I was that awkward girl in the corner who everyone hated. It didn't help that my father was the headmaster, but it didn't stop me from dreaming. Jack was that dream and when he asked me out, I couldn't agree quickly enough. Sad really, that despite everything, I'm still that awkward girl looking for acceptance."

Aunt Alice takes my hand and smiles sweetly. "Why do you think he asked you, Nelly?"

Feeling ashamed to admit the truth, I almost can't look at her. She is being so kind and here we are deceiving her. It's too much for me and I can't lie to a person I am fast gaining respect for, so I say sadly, "Probably because I have something he wants and he's using me to get it."

She stares at me sharply and says in a tight voice, "Explain."

I shrug miserably. "I'm not silly, Aunt Alice. Jack could have his pick of any girl in the county, but for some reason, he asked me. I think it has something to do with my business. Maybe I give him respectability and something he's never had before."

She raises her eyes, "What?"

I grin. "A challenge. I'm not the sort who will give into him. I call him out when he annoys me, and I don't think the sun shines from his backside."

I say conspiratorially, "Don't tell him this, but when I was in his class at school, I really fancied him. You know, like obsessive. He never knew I existed and so it's that girl who said yes, even though the grown-up part of me should have said no."

Her eyes soften and she squeezes my shoulder, saying kindly, "We've all been that girl, Nelly. In his defence, Jack's a kind boy at heart. I'm pretty sure he's not as shallow as you think he is. Give it time and you may be surprised. Life has a habit of making the extraordinary reality. I should know. My life has been charmed and I want that for my family. You may have heard that I set them all challenges."

I tense as I feel the flush taking over my face, but she either doesn't notice or ignores it and whispers, "Amanda and James need to reconnect. They have grown apart and nothing brings a couple closer than dancing. Well, outside of sex, of course."

She winks and I grin as she rolls her eyes. "Ariadne needs to learn humility and to learn that there are people with amazing stories to tell. She doesn't see real life and is dismissive of people who she considers beneath her. The care home was my way of placing her outside her comfort zone."

She smiles and I say nervously, "Why are you telling me this?"

She grins. "Because I like you. I knew as soon as laid eyes on you that you weren't the usual girl Jack dated. There's something about you that reminds me of myself, and I want you to know why I have done this. Jack's business was his idea. He always knew I wanted a shop of my own and maybe he thought it would make me look more favourably on him as a result. Possibly he asked you out for the same reason, but we'll give him the benefit of the doubt. However, when I saw the look he gave you when you left that room, I saw something I haven't seen before, which is why I'm telling you this."

My heart starts beating madly and I say nervously, "What did you see?"

She grins. "I saw the look. You know, the one when a man realises he has found something so precious, he can't quite believe it. The one where a man is wondering what's going on because he's feeling something he never has before. An awakening, a realisation, who knows what it is, but it's there, Nelly. You may question his motives and I'm not surprised by them, but one thing I can guarantee is that Jack is learning a valuable lesson here and that's all down to you."

She glances at the tray and smiles.

"We should be getting back so I can have my fun. Don't worry about the rest of them because underneath it all, they're good people. Life has a habit of making us forget what's important and hopefully, by the end of all this, they will find it again."

As I follow Aunt Alice back to the others, the only comment I can focus on is the one about the look in Jack's eyes. Surely not, she must be mistaken because Jack Mason has made no secret of the fact that this is a brief moment when our lives cross paths. She's delusional if she thinks it's anything more than that.

* * *

LATER, after dinner, we sit in the living room and Aunt Alice says to Amanda, "Tell me about the salsa lessons. Are they going well?"

Amanda smiles politely. "Yes, they seem to be going ok, but we still have quite a way to go before we're ready to enter the competition."

Aunt Alice grins. "Why don't you show us how it's done?"

Amanda and James look uncomfortable, but the glint in Aunt Alice's eyes makes them stand and demonstrate a few dance moves. It all seems a little odd because they have no music to follow, and it's strange watching them holding each other stiffly as they go through the motions. Jack and Ariadne look bored, and I see a thoughtful look on Aunt Alice's face as they move around the room, trying not to look annoyed.

When they finish, Amanda says brightly, "As you can see, we need lots of practice, but it's still early days."

Suddenly, she looks across at me and says loudly, "I forgot to say, Nelly, we met a couple last week who said they know you."

I stare at them with apprehension as James says, "Yes, that's right, a strange couple."

Amanda nods. "Yes, the guy was ok, but that woman was weird."

Jack stares at me nervously and I feel myself blushing as they describe what must be my parents. Amanda shares a look with James. "It was a bit awkward when that woman grabbed you during the lady's choice period. I must say, she wasn't very subtle about it. Her partner appeared as embarrassed as you were."

James pulls a face. "She was a bit keen. I felt sorry for her partner. She even asked if I could help her outside of the class. She tried to take my mobile number, saying we should meet up."

My face is burning as Jack says in surprise, "Do you know their names?"

Amanda shrugs. "I think she was called Vicky or something."

James interrupts, "No, it was Violet. That's it, Violet and I think the man was called Ken."

Now they have my full attention and I say quickly, "Ken's my landlord. How did they know that I knew you?"

James shrugs. "She mentioned she lived above the chocolate shop in town, and I asked if they knew you."

At least it wasn't my parents, but I cringe as I think of Ken with Violet. I don't know why, but there is something I don't like about her. Luckily, they change the subject as Aunt Alice wants to hear about the care home and I tune out as Ariadne fills her in.

Jack whispers, "Are you ok? You've gone quiet."

Lowering my voice, I say firmly, "There's something weird going on with Ken. He's left his long-standing girlfriend to go out with Violet. He even asked her to marry him after just a couple of weeks of dating. It's all happened so fast, and it's unlike him."

Jack nods. "Maybe it's what happens when you find the

right one. From what you say, he's older and maybe he's determined not to waste a minute. It could have been love at first sight."

I don't respond because I still don't believe it. Something isn't adding up and I'm determined to find out what it is.

CHAPTER 24

A few days later, I look up as the door opens and see Ken's new girlfriend standing there. She stares at me with a hard expression and heads towards the counter. Plastering a smile on my face, I say politely, "May I help you?"

She gazes around her irritably and shakes her head. "You can start by paying the rent you owe for last month."

"Excuse me."

Her eyes flash and she hisses, "Ken told me you were one month behind. He said it didn't matter, but I disagree. You see, I have his best interests at heart, and you are taking advantage of his generous nature."

I say haughtily, "That's none of your business. I deal with Ken and if he has a problem with it, he can come to me himself."

Violet shakes her head. "That's where you're wrong. You see, when we marry, I will be equal partners with him. We have discussed it and I am taking over the business side of things. So, you see, ultimately, I'm your new landlady and I am not offering you any extensions. So, pay what you owe otherwise you have notice to vacate the premises. Oh, and just to inform you, the rent will be going up. I will put it in writing, but I thought I'd forewarn you."

She peers around her disdainfully. "Remember what I've said because I'm no pushover. This is a business after all and not pleasure. I expect the payment by early next week. If you don't pay up, you will receive notice to leave."

Without waiting for a reply, she turns away and heads outside, leaving me speechless.

I'm still standing there when a welcome face heads through the door and Richie says loudly, "Good god, Nelly, has someone died or did you suddenly realise you're wearing Primark?"

I look at him in horror. "Something's happened and I don't know what to do about it."

He looks excited. "Ooh, I love a good drama. What is it? Did Jack ask you to join a threesome? I wouldn't be surprised, or maybe you've discovered he's gay and need me to check if it's true. I'm hoping for the latter, of course, but either way, I'm interested."

I stare at him in horror and the mask slips, and he looks concerned for once. "Come on honey, tell your uncle Richie."

I fill him in on what happened and by the end of it, his expression matches mine. "The vile cow. Let me have a word with her and bitch slap her into next week."

Groaning, I say sadly, "If it was only that simple. What am I going to do?"

He leans on the counter and shakes his head. "I'm not sure. I mean, really, you should have a word with Ken and tell him what she said. I'm sure he would be horrified."

"I doubt it. I am behind with the rent and maybe it's his way of making me pay. He's always been kind and patient, but perhaps it was all an act."

Richie shakes his head. "No way. Ken is probably as much a victim of this horror as you are. We need a cunning plan."

Sighing, I nod in agreement. "You're right. Maybe I should think of one because I can't afford the rent I owe, let alone an increase. I'll be out of business within the month and have to get a proper job like everyone else."

Shaking myself, I turn to Richie and try to change the subject. "So, how are things with you?"

He shrugs. "Same old. Roger is still acting the man patient and my patience is wearing as thin as a man's hair of a certain age. What I need is a holiday, preferably away from him."

"Why don't you both go? He could use the recuperation and it might make you both happier?"

Nodding, he smiles happily. "You could be right. Maybe I'll look into it. We could head to Disney World. Now he's in a temporary wheelchair we could go to the front of all the rides. Maybe he could be useful for once."

He grins. "So, problems aside, how are things going with the delectable Jack?"

"Fine, I guess."

"You guess? What's that supposed to mean?"

I stare across the road gloomily and catch Jack laughing at yet another group of adoring fans. "You know, Richie, there's a reason why women like me don't go out with men like Jack."

"Explain."

"Because we will never be enough."

He follows my gaze and registers the show opposite and shakes his head with disapproval. "You're wrong, Nelly. I think it's the other way around. Men like Jack never find the gold-plated relationship because they are blinded by the fake. Real gold is tarnished and dull but lasts the test of time. The glittery, fake, man-made jewels start off fabulous but tarnish damn quickly and get cast aside for the next new shiny toy. Pretty soon it all becomes vulgar and like a bad fashion mistake of the past. True gold increases in value and outshines any man-made copy. You are that gold, Nelly, and those girls are mere fashion items. One day, men like Jack will realise the value of you and treat you like the precious gem you are."

I grin. "Are you saying I'm like a tarnished lump of old metal? Thanks, I feel much better. I'm so glad I'm not considered a dazzling jewel of the utmost desirability instead."

Richie winks and slams a few bags of chocolate malted balls on the counter. "Check me out honey because I have a holiday to book."

By the time he leaves, I feel a little better, but the problem is still there. In fact, both problems are still there because not only am I about to lose my business, but it appears I'm about to lose my heart as well.

Over the next few days, I try every trick in the book to reach Ken. I spy from the window, waiting to see if Violet leaves without him. I try phoning the flat upstairs but hang up as soon as she answers. I've even sent Angela to knock on their door pretending to be from the council, but it's as if Ken has disappeared off the planet. I do, however, see him on the odd occasion leaving with Violet. Her hand is always possessively in his and she is all over him like a rash. The deadline is looming for the rent, and I'm getting desperate.

So, it's the last thing I need when Jack invites me over for a family supper to celebrate Aunt Alice's birthday. Apparently, she's coming to stay for a few days, so they can show her how they're progressing.

Since we went to her home, I haven't seen that much of Jack other than through my spy mirror. We've both been busy with work, and he heads to the gym most evenings after we close. If anyone asks, we say we meet up afterwards, but it's just another lie and I'm beginning to think that the moments I shared with Jack were just to get me to agree to this charade. He has kept his distance and for some reason, it bothers me way more than it should. He still brings me the odd coffee over but again, it's just for appearance's sake and so, call me an idiot, but I make an extra effort with my appearance tonight.

When will I ever learn?

CHAPTER 25

Tonight, I have pulled out all the stops and hate myself for it. I'm now that stupid fool who thinks she has a chance with the popular guy from class, despite the fact he's made it pretty clear what this is.

However, I am pleased with how I look as I have curled my hair in those giant rollers I got for Christmas and applied my make-up courtesy of a YouTube video. Ariadne will be so proud of me for that one. I didn't have much choice in the wardrobe department, so have resorted to some smart black jeans and a white silk blouse with a peplum jacket, also white. Silver costume jewellery reinforces Richie's comment on shiny fake things, and that's fine by me. This whole situation is fake anyway, so I may as well play the part.

When Jack arrives to pick me up, I am rewarded by the slightly stunned expression on his face as his eyes rake over me from head to toe. He almost can't find words, so I say flippantly, "Are you ready?"

He nods and I follow him outside to the waiting car.

I'm not sure why, but my nerves are all over the place tonight. Maybe it's because Jack looks good enough to eat in smart jeans and a tight-fitting top, or is it the aftershave he's wearing that's causing my mind to wander into unfamiliar territory? However, it's probably just the tight ball of nerves that has sat inside me ever since Violet strode into my shop with her demands.

We are both oddly quiet as we begin the journey and it must be twenty minutes later that Jack says slightly nervously, "Is everything ok, Nelly?"

I notice a genuine concern in his eyes and shrug. "I think so. Why, what's the matter?"

"I'm not sure, but you've seemed quite distant lately, and I was wondering if it was anything I've done to upset you."

I stare at him in shock. Me? Distant?

I shrug. "I don't know what you mean. To be honest, I haven't seen much of you except the odd cup of coffee here and there. From the looks of things, your um, customers have been keeping you quite busy and to my knowledge, you've just been heading to the gym after work. You must forgive me if I'm supposed to have done something. After all, this relationship charade is all new to me and I don't appear to have received my part of the script."

He stares at me with surprise. "To be honest, Nelly, I've kept away because you seemed preoccupied with something. The odd occasions I came over you seemed distracted and, well… not very interested if I'm honest. I thought maybe you were having second thoughts after spending that dreadful day with my family and maybe once you met Aunt Alice, you wanted to pull out. You were so quiet on the journey home, I was afraid to ask."

I can't believe what I'm hearing and see the genuine concern in his eyes. Relaxing slightly, I say sadly, "To be honest, I did have second thoughts when I met Aunt Alice. I liked her and it felt wrong deceiving her. However, something she said made me reconsider my options, so no, that's not why I've been quiet."

Sighing, I look down and say wearily, "No, my problems are now bigger than this charade we've fallen into. That woman your parents were talking about marched into my shop today and acted like some sort of mafia boss. Apparently, when she marries Ken, she will take over the running of the business and wants to increase my rent. She has also demanded last month's rent, even though Ken has always said it doesn't matter if I'm a little late with it. To be honest, I can't think of anything else because the way things are going, my business could be closed within a few months."

To my surprise, Jack reaches out and puts his hand on my knee and for a minute I just stare at it, thinking how good it looks there. Then he says in a calm, reassuring voice. "We'll work it out, don't worry."

I gaze up at him in surprise and see a softness in his eyes that mesmerises me. He almost looks as if he cares, which takes my breath away. Fighting the urge to cover his hand with mine, I smile weakly, "Thanks. I need all the friends I can get at the moment."

He smiles softly, "Well, I am your boyfriend, after all. Nobody messes with my girl and gets away with it."

He winks and I almost pass out. His girl. If only it were true.

* * *

I'M nervous as we head inside Jacks parent's house because this family scares me on every level. Tonight, the house is bathed in candlelight, and I briefly wonder if it's legal to have this many open flames around so many reed diffusers. What if they ignite the vapour or something? Aunt Alice's birthday would go up like a firework.

As expected, everyone looks as if they have just dressed for the Oscars, and I feel like blending into the furnishings. Amanda is wearing a red silk dress and her lips are painted to match. James looks like the man from the aftershave ad that sends me delirious every time I see it and Aunt Alice is immaculate in a white shift dress with pearls and a pashmina draped elegantly over her shoulders. When she sees us coming, her smile is genuine, and she heads towards us holding out her arms. "Nelly, my dear, how lovely you look. It's good to see you again."

She envelops me in her perfumed embrace, and I'm tempted to stay there for a minute in the security of her arms. However, politeness dictates my moves and I pull back and offer her the larger box of chocolates I selected, along with the birthday card I bought for her. She looks absolutely delighted, although I'm sure she's used to much more extravagant gifts and says happily, "Chocolates are always my favourite gift. Let me put them somewhere safe so I can gorge on them in private later."

She winks and heads off to her room and Amanda snaps, "Jack, fix Nelly a drink and James, please take her coat. Goodness, the men in this house must always be told."

I'm slightly embarrassed as I shrug out of my jacket and hand it to James, who smiles charmingly. "You look lovely, Nelly."

I feel myself blushing as I register that my jacket looks like a rag in his hand and take a few deep, calming, zen breaths to help me through. Ariadne and Godfrey are taking selfies as usual, and I can see why. They are such a dream couple. She is wearing a tight-fitting, silver bodycon dress and her hair is curled way more professionally than mine. The hands that hold the camera reveal the most amazing set of silver nails I have ever seen. Her make-up is like something out of a magazine, and she could be the model she so aspires to be.

Godfrey looks amazing in black trousers and a crisp white shirt with a jacket that makes him appear smart and affluent.

His hair is slicked back for once and he is every inch a successful businessman, which makes me wonder what he actually does for a living. They see me watching them and Ariadne smiles, beckoning me over.

"Hi Nelly, I don't suppose you could take a few photos of us, could you?"

Nodding, I take the phone from her hands and start snapping away as they pose for the camera. I must hand it to them. They are good. Every frame resembles something from the red carpet, and I resist the urge to add one of those animal filters just to mess them up a bit. It's not fair that two people could look so good all the time.

After what feels like hundreds of poses later, I hand the phone back and she pounces on it like an oxygen mask in a decompression. Squealing, she scrolls through, saying at random. "No, this won't do, ugh, I had my eyes closed in this one, hm this one may be of use. Godfrey, you look like an idiot in this one. Yes, this could work, hm, not so sure about this one. Oh, you got mum's arm in this one. I think I have a filter that could work with this one…"

I tune out as the conversation begins to irritate me, and Jack hands me a large glass of wine. "Here you go, something to get you through the ordeal."

We wander over to the side of the room and Jack lowers his voice. "Listen, Nelly, I just wanted to say…."

"May I have your attention, please?"

We look up to see Amanda clapping her hands and calling the room to attention. She turns to James and nods, saying, "James, please light the candles. We need to present Aunt Alice with her cake."

Feeling worried about the fact he is now lighting another shed load of candles to add to St Elmo's fire, we all start singing Happy Birthday. Aunt Alice beams around at us all and claps her hand with delight when James presents the burning cake to her as she attempts to blow out the equivalent of a bush fire on the serving dish before her. Everyone claps as she makes it by the tenth attempt, and she laughs happily.

"Thank you, everyone, for making my birthday so exciting. We don't spend much time together, so I value any we do. I'm aware that circumstances are a little different this year and I have set you some interesting challenges. I hope they haven't been too difficult, and I'll look forward to seeing the results in a few months' time."

One by one, everyone claps and then heads over to kiss her on the cheek.

As they drift off back to what they were doing, Jack takes my arm and propels me outside the room, away from the noise, and I gaze at him with surprise. He stands looking a little awkward and I say, "What's the matter? Is something wrong?"

He shakes his head and says hesitantly, "Um... well... I just wanted to warn you that I may do the odd strange... um... boyfriend thing this evening. I don't want Aunt Alice to suspect anything, so do you mind if I occasionally hold your hand or, um... kiss you a little?"

Trying hard not to let my excitement show, I nod coolly. "If you think it would help, of course."

He steps closer and I hold my breath as he reaches up and pulls me close. "Um... what are you doing, Jack? There's nobody here."

He whispers, "I think we should practise, don't you?"

OK, this is unexpected and, feeling as if Christmas has come early, I whisper, "We've practised before. Why now?"

His eyes sparkle and I lose my mind in them as he says huskily, "Because I want to."

He wants to kiss me. Why?

However, I don't have time to dissect the intentions behind the request because, as if in slow motion, I see those heavenly lips heading my way. The nerves start fluttering like butterflies in my stomach as he advances slowly towards me. I don't even have time to lick my lips before his is on mine and it's a glorious feeling.

This kiss with Jack is different. Somehow, it's more intimate and secret. We are standing in his parent's home like a normal couple, and he has spirited me away to have his wicked way with me out of sight of prying eyes.

Forgetting myself, I kiss him back with everything I've got. I'm not one to look a gift horse in the mouth and so I allow myself to indulge in my fantasy for once. This time the kiss lasts longer and reaches a whole new level and in my mind we are a couple, and this is what we do all the time.

Jack twists my hair and holds my head in place as he devours me like a hungry beast. We press closer and our bodies are touching and I'm sure he can feel the thump of my beating wanton heart as I press my body against his. Somewhere from the back of my subconscious, I hear a groan and hope to God it isn't me, but then I don't care anymore because this is the stuff of fairy tales.

Suddenly, we hear, "Oh for god's sake, Jack, couldn't you wait? Mum wants us to watch Aunt Alice open her presents."

We quickly pull apart and I see Ariadne looking at us with amusement from the doorway and I blush. Jack just smiles. "We'll be there in a second."

She heads off murmuring, and Jack throws me a sexy look and whispers, "Thanks for that. You know, you surprise me more every minute I spend with you. I'm glad you're my girlfriend."

He winks as he pulls me back into the kitchen, leaving me one big, hot mess. This man is good. He messes with women's minds and strips them of all rational thought. If I didn't know better, I would really believe he meant every word he just said.

* * *

It's great fun watching Aunt Alice open her presents. None of the usual flowers and boxed soaps for her, instead Amanda and James have bought her a spa day for two in a nearby exclusive resort. Ariadne and Godfrey have bought her a paint balling day out for her, and three friends and Jack gave her a Victoria Secret's voucher. I'm ashamed at my own lack of originality when faced with these amazing thoughts and as she catches my eye, she smiles and says gratefully, "And, of course, Nelly bought me the most amazing box of chocolates. Obviously, she knew the real way to my heart."

I smile, but it's laced with anxiety, and she picks up on it immediately.

"What's the matter, darling? You look a little subdued."

All eyes swivel in my direction and I say sadly, "I had a visit from a most unpleasant woman and I'm still working out what to do about it."

Amanda says sharply, "Tell us, maybe we can be of some help."

Jack says bitterly, "It's that woman who was after dad in the salsa class. Apparently, when she marries the man she was with, she will become Nelly's new landlady. She has already demanded rent with menaces and promised an increase. It's no wonder Nelly's upset."

Amanda shakes her head and says tightly, "I told you she wasn't to be trusted, didn't I, James? She had that predatory look of a woman out on a gold rush."

Aunt Alice looks thoughtful. "So, business is slow, and you are worrying about making the rent?"

I nod miserably and she stares at Jack with interest. "Do you think this is something you've caused by opening?"

He nods. "I don't think I've helped the situation. Maybe we should pool our resources and try to bolster Nelly's trade."

Ariadne shakes her head. "You can try that if you like, but I always think you should fight fire with fire. Don't be a pushover and fight back."

Jack rolls his eyes. "This isn't the playground, you know, Ariadne. This is a grown-up problem and needs to be dealt with accordingly."

She glares at him irritably. "Think about it, Jack. She's obviously in this for the money. This man, whoever he is, is being manipulated and played. Well, it's up to us to show him the error of his ways and get her shoved back from where she came from."

Godfrey says in confusion, "What can we do, sugar pie? By the sounds of it, this woman isn't one to go lightly. No, my advice would be for Nelly to pay up and then look for another vacant unit in the town. She is best showing that she can walk away elsewhere."

We all look at him and shout simultaneously, "Shut up, Godfrey!"

He frowns as Aunt Alice nods enthusiastically. "I agree with Ariadne. She's picked the wrong family to mess with. We don't take kindly to idle threats, and now it's our mission to bring her down. Let's put our heads together to think of the best way to achieve it. Don't worry, Nelly, we'll make sure your problem goes away if it's the last thing we do."

CHAPTER 26

By the time Jack and I leave, we have a thin outline of a plan and I'm doubtful it will work and could make the whole situation much worse. However, that's not my only problem because Jack's acting strangely, and I'm not sure why. I know we had to keep up the pretence in front of his family, but he appears to have forgotten they're not here. For the entire journey, he reaches for my hand on the odd occasion and squeezes it. He makes plans for me to come over and watch the new series on Netflix we both liked the look of, and he asked me if I fancied joining him after work at the gym one evening for a workout.

After a while, I say firmly, "What's going on, Jack?"

He sounds surprised. "What do you mean?"

"All of this. The plans, the loving touches, the shared nights ahead. It's all a bit excessive, if you ask me."

He says tightly, "I'm just playing my part, Nelly."

"Hm, a little too well, if you ask me. Listen, I promise I won't pull out. Is that it? Do you think you need to persuade me to stay to keep up the pretence? I know I told you I'd had second thoughts, but quite honestly, I'm too exhausted, emotionally speaking, to care anymore. We can continue with this charade until you get your money and then maybe I'll get mine."

I didn't mean to be so hard and brutal, and as soon as the words leave my mouth, I regret them. The atmosphere in the car changes to an icy one and he says tightly, "Of course, the money. After all, that is what we agreed."

I feel terrible but just shrug. "It was your idea, not mine. You talked me into it and, quite honestly, I knew you would struggle with it. What's the matter? Are you feeling bereft of female company and have now resorted to hitting on the hired help?"

I wish I could sew my mouth together because what is spilling out is vitriol, even to my own ears. I suppose all the hurt, resentment, rejection, and recent threats have tainted my mind because I have absolutely no self-worth left and no self-esteem.

Jack doesn't answer and just screeches into the visitor's bay near my apartment and says in a cold voice, "Fine. If that's all this is to you, then maybe we should take any emotion out of it. You have made it perfectly clear you are only doing a job and want nothing else from me. I'll let you know when we need to venture out in public, but until then, have a nice night."

I open my mouth to speak, but his furious expression silences me. I've upset him, it's obvious. He is trying to mask it, but I see real hurt in his eyes, and he appears upset. He scowls and nods towards the door. "Go on then."

Feeling like a complete bitch, I open the door and say in a small voice, "I'm sorry. I didn't mean to say those things. You've only been nice to me, and I've just thrown it all back in your face. I wouldn't blame you if you wanted nothing more to do with me. I'm sorry, Jack."

I make to leave before the tears arrive and am surprised when a hand pulls me back and a voice says gently, "Don't go."

Spinning around, I'm surprised to see his expression has changed to one I know all too well. The look of loneliness.

He smiles shakily. "I'm sorry. I have something I need to tell you, and you aren't going to like it."

My heart starts beating so fast I can almost hear it and I say fearfully, "What is it?"

He looks down and says in a small voice, "Can I come in?"

Nodding, I exit the car and it's as if I'm about to experience one of those moments in life when everything changes. The crossroads that determines the path to tread and a parting of the ways, or another journey into the unknown together.

Whatever Jack is about to say is serious, judging by his expression and I'm not sure that today, of all days, I'm ready to hear what it is.

We head into my flat and I don't even register the usual mess that greets us. Something is happening here, and it's serious. I try to lighten the atmosphere and say nervously, "Um... would you like a coffee, tea, hot chocolate or maybe something stronger?"

He shakes his head and stands awkwardly in the doorway. I shrug and say nervously, "Ok, then... um... you had better tell me what's on your mind then."

He takes a deep breath and says in a low voice, "I suppose I had better start with what happened today and work backwards."

Now I'm confused and just nod as he sighs heavily. "Emma told me something that made me mad."

My heart thumps as I wonder what she said and shrug, "So what? Emma's always been a gossip and a bitch. Surely you take whatever she says with a pinch of salt."

He fixes with me a severe look and I wonder what on earth

she told him because to my knowledge it's nothing I could have done?

He says tightly, "It was just after we locked up. She asked me how things were going with us, and I said fine. She seemed nervous and shy, which isn't like her, and it made me curious. She appeared worried and said she'd heard a rumour about you and hadn't wanted to say anything, but she cared too much for me to see me made a fool of."

I'm not sure what I should say because so far none of this is ringing any bells with me, so I shrug, "What am I supposed to have done, or said for that matter?"

"She told me your friend Angela told her you were well known for being a little over-friendly with your reps. Apparently, they all loved coming to see you because you sampled more than their chocolates in the back room of your shop."

I can't help it and burst out laughing. "Seriously! You are kidding me."

One look at his expression tells me he's not, and he says gruffly, "She also said that the woman who threatened you had found out you were after her fiancé and had propositioned him. She told her that you were well known for being easy and she didn't want me to be made to look like a fool."

I feel the disappointment forming a huge knot inside my stomach as I say angrily, "And you believe her, of course."

Jack moves across and pulls me towards him with one sudden move that makes me wonder if he's about to murder me. Instead, there's a fierce look in his eyes as he almost shouts, "Of course I don't believe her. What do you take me for?"

I stare at him with the utmost confusion. "Then what's the problem?"

He almost shouts. "You are the problem, Nelly. You! Do you know what she did after she told me?"

I shake my head, wondering if he's gone a little mad as he

shouts, "She kissed me. She pressed her body against mine and kissed me, telling me that she had always loved me and girls like you didn't deserve men like me. She told me we were always meant to be together, and I never saw what was staring at me in the face all those years."

He breaks off and says roughly, "And she was right."

My voice shakes as I say, "She was?"

He nods. "But it wasn't her staring at me in the face… it was you."

"Me!"

His face softens and my breath hitches when I see the emotion in his eyes. "As soon as she said the words, everything clicked into place. The way my heart lifted when I saw you staring at me through that window. You may have changed a lot since school, but I knew it was you. It took me back to those days where you were just another girl in class. The girl we all disregarded, yet for some inexplicable reason, always made me look twice. There was always something about you that drew my attention, and I never knew why. I thought it was because you were odd and a little strange. Maybe out of reach because you were the headmaster's daughter and off limits. But when I saw you again, it all came flooding back. Maybe I had an epiphany because I couldn't pass by the chance to get to know you better."

I stare at him in total shock. This was not what I expected to hear. He smiles nervously. "Look at you. You're clever, beautiful and well out of my league. You also appeared to hate me and when you wouldn't come to my opening, I was surprised. Then when you did and confronted the group from school, it turned my world around. You see, Nelly, I have been trying to figure out why I'm so uncharacteristically drawn to you, and it's taken me a long time to realise that…"

I hold my breath as he says softly, "It was always going to be you."

For a moment, I just stare at him. He spoke, and I heard what I thought were words I have dreamt of hearing spilling from his lips, but the reality must be very different because guys like Jack don't say those words to girls like me. He pulls me beside him on the couch and says in a worried voice. "The trouble is, I have done something you may not be able to forgive."

A sense of dread creeps over me. Of course, here it is, the sting in the tail. Whatever brief moment of magic just happened is about to turn to dust, because I know that look in his eyes. I'm about to get the killer statement that ends this before it's even begun.

He shakes his head and says in a small voice, "I lied."

I whisper, "About what?"

"The challenge."

My mind struggles to keep up, as I say with confusion. "No, you didn't. Your aunt told me herself she had set you challenges."

He grins sheepishly. "She did. The shop was mine."

I nod. "Yes, the shop. You needed to open a business from scratch and keep the same girlfriend for the rest of the year."

He laughs nervously, "The shop was my challenge. The girl was never part of it."

I stare at him in astonishment. "Then why…?"

"Because I wasn't lying when I asked you to be my girl-friend. Then when we went on the date and it all became real, it made me nervous. I started to worry that I wasn't ready. Maybe you weren't the one for me and I was just chasing the impossible. Then when you were about to walk away, I panicked and so I stretched my aunt's challenge to give me some time. I would persuade you to help me by offering to pay your rent. That way, it would make you dislike me a little less for opening opposite and give me some breathing space to see if this was what I thought it was."

"Breathing space?"

"I'm sorry, Nelly. I've misled you and spun such a web I'm starting to be trapped in my own lies. It changed when I heard what happened today. It made me sick to my stomach, and I wanted to march over there and tear those people limb from limb. You were upset, so I was upset. When you told me we were just pretending, I realised I didn't want you to think that way anymore. I want to be the guy who stands beside you, who you turn to for everything. I want us to be a team like your parents are and I think this could be the start of something life changing. But I can't base it all on a lie. It's one thing wanting someone, but it won't work if they don't feel the same."

The silence sits between us as we allow the words to sink in. Jack likes me as a man likes a woman. Me! Nelly Gray!

I stare at him in shock, and he smiles gently. Then he takes me by surprise and drops to the floor on one knee and says loudly, "Nelly Gray, will you be my girlfriend... for real this time?"

* * *

THERE IS that moment in life that you have heard a thousand times before in your dreams. When the prince asks the princess to marry him. When Danny chooses Sandy and doesn't care what people think. When good conquers evil and when the meaning of life is revealed. This is that moment for me. The past now makes sense and reveals the path to the future. Past disappointments and betrayals cease to matter because it all becomes clear. Life's tapestry begins to take shape and the puzzle pieces finally fit. There really is no other word to say than, "Yes, Jack. I'll be your girlfriend... for real... um... but only if that is really what you..."

My word is captured at the back of his throat as he kisses

me hard, demanding and in ownership. This kiss seals our future and changes everything. Jack and Nelly have made it through every obstacle thrown in their way because they finally found their way home. At least that's what I like to believe.

CHAPTER 27

It's weird how life turns out. Here I was, totally obsessing that I wasn't good enough for the school heartthrob and he was doing the same over the nerd.

For the next few days, I am walking on air and any problems I have are firmly pushed away because I intend on savouring every moment of my new relationship. I can't even tell my friends because they already think we're a couple – oh, the irony.

Instead, Jack and I take the time to pull down the barriers and really get to know one another. We spend the evenings watching Netflix or going to the gym. I'm not even bothered that we're spending too much time with each other because why pretend? That's what started this whole fiasco off and if we'd been honest from the start, we would have saved a lot of wasted time.

I think Jack and I only stop kissing to breathe and eat. Occasionally, we catch what the movie is about, but I can't remember what we have actually watched. The gym sessions are just an excuse to stare unashamedly at each other as we practise our moves and the hot flushes I endure have nothing to do with nature. No, life is good except for one thing and that thing rears its ugly head when I'm least expecting it.

As I sort through the caramel kisses, I hear the door chime and look up. However, my welcome smile freezes when I see Violet glaring at me with hostility. She glances around her disdainfully and says angrily, "I don't appear to have your rent as agreed. I'm here to collect it in person."

Slowly, I walk over to the cash register and open it with a flourish and withdraw an envelope from inside. I push a receipt book towards her and say firmly, "Your rent is all here, and I require your signature as proof it has been paid."

Sneering, she takes the envelope from my outstretched fingers and rips it open greedily. She withdraws the cheque made out to Ken and her eyes flash. "In the future, we would prefer cash."

I say nothing and just hand her the pen and the book, and she grabs it roughly from my fingers and scrawls an illegible signature across the page.

I say firmly, "Please print your name so it can be recognised."

She huffs, "Is this strictly necessary?"

I say nothing and she takes the pen and angrily prints her name. As she straightens up, I say icily, "Now, if I may ask you to leave, I have work to do."

Shrugging, she turns to leave, and I say loudly, "Oh, I almost forgot."

As she turns, I withdraw another envelope and hold it towards her. "Just a few repairs I need to be carried out before the next rent cheque is due. The damp is coming in again from the flat upstairs and has marked the carpet. Obviously, I sell food, so hygiene is involved and, as my landlords, you are responsible for the maintenance of the building. Now, I used to just deal with this sort of thing myself, but as we are now doing things properly, I would like that to apply to my rights as well.

I'm sure there are more things to put right and will draw up my list before the next cheque is due. Good day."

The look she shoots me makes my heart sing as she storms from the shop. Yes, Violet is about to learn just what being a landlord involves. I feel a pang when I think about Ken hearing about my demands. It's true, I never bothered him with the little things, and he always let me off other things. It was a good working relationship that suited us both until Violet arrived. Maybe if he came and spoke to me, we could work things out. However, all my requests have been ignored, so now I have no choice.

Despite my small victory, it's a hollow one. I want my friend back, not this… person who has taken his place. Sadly, I wonder if that's possible now.

CHAPTER 28

Thursday night and I can't quite believe we're here. As Jack and I stand hand in hand outside Cilla's Salsa at the Armitage Centre, my nerves threaten to call this whole thing off. I still can't quite believe we're doing this, and that Jack even agreed to it, but here we are, about to enrol in the same class Amanda and James attend.

I peer at Jack and say in a small voice, "Are you sure about this?"

He squeezes my hand and says firmly, "Of course."

We share a look and then head inside to try to put things right.

Cilla Barnes is the lady we need to see, and there are no prizes for guessing who she is. As soon as we step foot inside the room, we hear a loud voice say, "Newbies, how fantastic! Come in, come in, don't stand on ceremony."

As our eyes adjust to the glare of the lights, we are amazed at the slightly disturbing sight of a mature woman dressed as a flamenco dancer bearing down on us. Her hair is wrapped in a scarf, and she has bright red painted lips and the bangles on her arms jangle as she moves. "Welcome, my dears, have you come to salsa?"

She performs a strange pirouette and stamps her feet as she laughs and I swallow hard. "Yes. We would like to learn."

"Bravo my darlings. Come into the light and let me see you."

She pulls us into the middle of the room and stares at us critically. "Hm, yes, a little stiff perhaps, but that's probably the nerves. Just follow the class and you'll soon pick it up."

She turns away to greet the next people through the door and Jack gazes around furtively. "Are they here yet?"

"Who, your parents or the targets?"

"The targets, of course. I think I'd know my own parents."

I glance around and spy Ken smooching in a corner with Violet and almost heave on the spot. "There they are. I can't believe they're all over each other in a public place."

Jack raises his eyes and grins and I feel myself turn red as I remember being caught doing much the same thing in the supermarket aisle yesterday when Jack and I went shopping after work. Shaking my head, I say crossly, "It's different. He should know better."

Luckily, Amanda and James arrive and head straight over to us. Amanda lowers her voice. "I can see you've located them. I mean, who wears orange - ever? The woman's a monster."

I'm inclined to agree with her because Violet is dressed head to toe in orange chiffon.

James smirks. "She resembles an amber traffic light, you know, the one that means ready."

Amanda rolls her eyes. "Yes, that's your favourite kind of signal."

He grins. "I'm not so sure. I quite like the green one."

Jack looks uncomfortable as his parents glare at one another and then luckily, Cilla claps her hands and calls everyone to attention. "Class, I have some exciting news.

Firstly, we must welcome some young blood into the fold. We have two new dancers among us."

She shines a torch on us, and we smile and try to shield our eyes as everyone claps. Then she says, "I have three spots to the regional finals up for grabs. You have just six weeks to convince me that I should put you through and the winner of the whole competition wins twenty thousand pounds. That's amazing news, isn't it?"

The class cheer and for some reason, I stare at Violet. Her eyes are gleaming, and she is speaking urgently to Ken.

Amanda whispers, "I'm not surprised she looks excited. Women like that are all about the money. Now she can fleece that poor man and use him to earn herself some extra cash. Shameless!"

Amanda's right because there's a look in Violet's eye that shouts determination. Poor Ken is about to spend the next six weeks of his life brushing up on his dancing skills because Violet is obviously a woman who doesn't like coming second.

The music starts and I'm slightly amused to watch James take Amanda in his arms as they start to follow the teacher. They look uncomfortable, and I wonder when things started to go so badly wrong for them. It's obvious they can't stand each other because I've never seen them share a memory or a warm look. All they share are recriminatory remarks and it's difficult to be around.

Jack pulls me close and whispers, "This is going to be fun."

I agree with him because any excuse to gyrate against Jack in public is worth all the effort we are going to put into this.

We spend the evening concentrating on everything we are told to do and despite it all, I am enjoying every minute of it. Jack's a fast learner and has surprised me with his skill on the dance floor. I never had him down as a dancer, more a footballer, but he is light on his feet and quick to move.

By the time we reach the break, my head is spinning with it

all, and I wonder why I never thought of this before. This is amazing.

As Jack heads off to grab us some refreshments, Violet stops by and sneers. "I know what you're up to."

I feign disinterest. "It's called dancing, Violet."

"Is that what you call your pathetic attempt to get Ken to talk to you? Well, he's sent me over to tell you to stay away."

Shrugging, I turn my back on her as Amanda heads over with James. The look Amanda throws Violet is priceless as she says loudly, "Oh, look darling, it's that woman from last week. You know, the desperate one who tried to get your number."

Violet storms off as James does a rare thing and laughs. "That told her. She really is so transparent. Why can't your friend see that for himself?"

I spy Ken carefully moving through the crowd, balancing two glasses of wine in his hands, and I feel a surge of affection for him. This isn't his fault. I know he's being fed all sorts of tales by Violet, and I just need a moment alone with him to set the record straight. Leaning towards Jack, who conveniently arrives with the drinks, I whisper, "I hope this works."

He laughs softly. "I'd bet my business on it."

We finally get our chance at the end of the evening when Cilla shouts, "Ok everyone, ladies' choice! Gentlemen, please line up on one side and ladies on the other."

I stand next to Amanda and pray this works out.

Cilla turns to me and says loudly, "Let our newest member select first."

I take a moment to glare triumphantly at Violet as I march over to Ken and say softly, "May I have the pleasure?"

He appears surprised and then a little hesitant, but there is nothing he can do without looking like a bad sport, so he smiles thinly and nods, casting a nervous look in Violet's direction. As the rest of the ladies choose, I notice that Violet chooses Jack and smile to myself. Of course she would.

As we take our positions, I say quietly, "We need to talk."

The music starts and I soon realise how difficult it is to have a serious conversation while salsa dancing. With every swing, sweep and move, my words are carried away over Ken's shoulders and I can't hear what he replies. After a while, I stop trying and just say loudly, "What's going on, Ken? I thought we were friends."

He shakes his head. "We are."

"Then why won't you take my calls or come and see me? Violet told me you wanted me to stay away, and she was dealing with things now."

He looks worried. "Listen, I'm sorry about that, but I had to let Violet take things off my hands for a while. To be honest, she has pointed out several things I've been doing wrong and has really made me sharpen up. It's nothing personal, just business."

I can't help myself and say tartly, "Is that what you texted Patty?"

He flinches and says in a low voice, "I deserved that."

"Maybe but she didn't. Have you even spoken to her once since you sent that message?"

He peers over his shoulder with a worried expression as Violet dances nearby and says in a dull voice, "It's complicated."

Sighing, I pull him closer and whisper, "Then try to get away and come and explain it to me tomorrow. This isn't the place, but I know a quieter one."

He smiles thinly and nods. "I'll see what I can do. No promises, though."

I notice Violet staring at us intently and swing around so we are obscured by another couple. As the music changes, it doesn't surprise me that she comes to claim her man and leads him away as if I'm contagious.

Jack pulls me into his arms as the song changes and whispers, "So, did you get to talk?"

"Not really, but he's promised to come and find me tomorrow. How about you? Did you find anything out?"

Jack grins wickedly. "A little. I've discovered Violet's a flirt and not averse to flattery. I've also extended an invitation to come and check out the competition tomorrow, so that may give you some breathing space with Ken."

I roll my eyes. "Of course, she'll want to visit on her own. What did you tempt her with?"

Laughing, he swings me around and dips me to the floor, whispering, "Aside from the fact that I'm totally irresistible, I may have said I was investing in a chain of More than Chocolates around the country. Her money grabbing eyes lit up like a firework, especially when I laid on the charm and made her think there was more than chocolate on offer, for her, anyway."

Despite the fact it's weird to be happy at the thought that your boyfriend has just propositioned the local harlot, I smile with approval. "Well done, Jack. I knew I could count on you."

Now the business of the evening has been done, we both just relax and enjoy the dancing. I never realised how much fun it could be, and I'm even surprised to see Amanda and James laughing at something in the corner. Maybe Aunt Alice has hit on something here. Spending time together in close proximity could be a blessing in disguise for the two of them.

CHAPTER 29

It's actually three days later when Ken edges into the shop and looks around him furtively.

"I haven't got long, Nelly. Violet's having a shower, so I said I'd pop out for a newspaper."

Quickly, I pull him inside and lock the door. "That should keep the non-existent customers out." I say lightly and drag him into the back room of the shop.

Ken holds up his hands and says with resignation. "Before you say anything, I know I was wrong. I should never have ended things with Patty the way I did, but Violet said it was the best way all round. She even drafted the text for me, and I was such a coward I went along with it."

I frown. "It was a despicable thing to do. Patty was devastated and probably still is. What made you do it in the first place?"

Ken sighs heavily. "I don't know what happened. As you know, Patty's sister came to stay, so I kept away for my own sanity. It's been a little rocky with Patty anyway because she spends so much time at the farm and is never around to do the things I want to. Well, I decided to try the salsa club and signed up for the lessons on the spot. I was paired with Violet, who kind of took my breath away."

His voice softens and his eyes sparkle as he says gently, "She was like a breath of fresh air. Young, beautiful, funny and can dance like a pro. What's more, she seemed to really like me and after class we went for a drink, and she never left."

He laughs at the shock on my face and grins. "I know, mad, isn't it? Anyway, I've never been a believer in love at first sight, until now. I can't get enough of Violet, and she moved in with me straight away. One thing led to another, and we started planning our future. She told me I could be earning lots more money than I do and drew up an impressive business plan. As a reward, I told her I'd make her an equal partner with me, and we would make our dreams come true together. So, you see, Nelly, it's nothing personal, but Violet is so much better at this than me. We decided to marry because I've discovered life's too short. I love her and she loves me, so why wait? Obviously, she's a lot younger and wants to start a family and, given my age, we need to get a move on if that dream stands a chance at becoming a reality. I feel bad about Patty, but when something's so right, how can it be wrong?"

The phrase 'stupid old fool' is screaming to be heard, but I hold it in. There's no point saying what I really think because it's obvious Ken's been brainwashed by this professional gold digger. So, instead, I just smile and say warmly, "I'm happy for you, Ken."

He looks surprised and then a quick glance at his watch has him jumping to his feet. "Thanks, Nelly, it means a lot. Now, I should be going because Violet doesn't want me coming down here. She says she needs to establish her position as the landlady and our friendship could get in the way of that. I think she's right, of course, so it's nothing personal, but I must stay away – for now, anyway."

As he turns to leave, I say after him, "I think you should call Patty, though. It's the least she deserves."

He shakes his head sadly. "I don't think I'm strong enough to do that yet. Call me a coward and a fool, but I just can't. Maybe she needs to hate me for what I've done to get over the situation quicker. It's for the best all round, really."

As he leaves the shop, I feel the frustration burning inside me. This is bad, very bad. Ken has been brainwashed in a matter of hours by a very clever adversary. I don't believe for one minute Violet is his soul mate. She's just a young woman ticking all the right boxes, leading a very gullible man down the garden path. Maybe it's time to step up my game because I am not going to let her win.

CHAPTER 30

The next few days pass uneventfully. Jack had his visit from Violet but had nothing to report back. Apparently, Emma took an instant dislike to her and spilt some coffee on Violet's new silk clutch bag, which made for an interesting spectacle. Despite the fact Emma tried to break up our fake relationship, I forgive her immediately for that act alone.

As I cash up at the end of yet another quiet day, I am excited about the evening ahead. Another night of salsa and we have everything to play for because Jack and I have decided to go all out for the competition. Not for the money, although I could certainly use a cash injection, it's because we want to annoy Violet by beating her to the prize. It was after Ken's visit that a plan began to take shape in my mind. It's a little far-fetched and relies on a chain of events to all work out perfectly, but it's worth a shot at least. If I have my way, by the end of the competition, Violet will be history.

***

However, just when you think things can't get any worse, they do.

As soon as we arrive, I notice a couple of familiar faces and my heart sinks. Nudging Jack, I whisper, "Don't look now, but my parents are over there."

Jack follows my gaze, and it may be my imagination, but he stands a little straighter and says seriously, "So they are. We should go over and say hello."

My heart sinks as I follow him, and my mother looks up and beams with excitement. "There you are. We had a spare evening, so we thought we would come and join you."

She says anxiously, "You don't mind, do you?"

We shake our heads dutifully, as my father says loudly, "Of course they mind. What kid wants their parents to gate crash their fun? I told you it wouldn't go down well."

Then we hear, "What won't go down well?"

I cringe as Amanda and James reach us and glance at my parents with interest. Jack says, "Mum, dad, meet Nelly's parents, um… Tom and Bettina."

My mother holds out her hand politely and shakes Amanda's hand and it strikes me how different they are. One, poised, elegant and chic and yet so cold she could freeze ice with just one sharp stare. The other, plain, dowdy and insignificant, yet the warmest person you could ever meet, and the funniest. Chalk and cheese and fire and ice on a collision course that I can't do a thing about.

Amanda raises a well-shaped eyebrow and says politely, "I'm pleased to meet you both. I'm Amanda, Jack's mother, and this is my husband James."

I watch as they all shake hands politely and then Cilla rescues the situation and says happily, "More new people, how amazing! Have you danced before?"

My parents share an excited look and my mother nods. "Yes, we were regional champions about twenty years ago.

We're a little rusty now though, and that was for ballroom as a whole, not salsa."

Cilla looks as if the gods have answered her prayers and gushes. "How amazing. You are most welcome to our humble classes… um… your majesties."

Jack snorts and I sense myself blushing as Amanda and James look on in shock. My parents just laugh, and mum says awkwardly. "We're not that good. As I said, it was a long time ago."

I catch sight of Ken and Violet in the corner and feel the irritation stir at the sight of her possessive hand on his arm as she scans the room. I watch her sizing up the competition and I'd like to think it was purely for dance purposes, however, I can tell it's the men she's scanning for, and it makes me so mad to think she's already planning Ken's replacement should a better option present itself.

Suddenly, my mother nudges my father and says in surprise, "Good god, is that Soraya?"

I follow her gaze and notice with a start she's talking about Violet. Amanda also hears and says with interest, "What, Violet? Do you know her?"

My mother appears confused. "Goodness, she looks exactly like that pupil you had to exclude a while ago, Tom."

My father screws up his eyes and peers into the gloom just as Violet sees them. I watch in fascination as she spins her back to us and my father shakes his head. "I don't think so. Last I heard, she'd moved to Norfolk. In fact, come to think of it, I'm sure she did because we had the details sent through."

My mother shrugs. "Well, I could have sworn it was her."

Amanda interrupts. "What did you say her name was?"

"Soraya Bellfield. She was a handful and tried to cause all sorts of problems for one of Tom's colleagues. He almost lost his job over her accusations."

Despite being the most interested I've ever been in hearing

one of my mother's stories, it will have to wait because Cilla claps her hands and calls the room to attention. "Let us begin."

For the next half an hour, we follow her lead, but my mind is buzzing with this new information. Jack is also thoughtful and whispers, "I think we should find out more about this Soraya person. If it is Violet, we may be able to prove she's up to no good and get her out of all our lives."

I whisper, "I had the same thought. Leave it with me. I'll find out what I can."

I notice that Violet keeps as far away from my parents as possible all evening, which tells me everything I need to know. This could be just the breakthrough we need.

* * *

AFTER CLASS, we find ourselves agreeing to share a pizza with our respective parents. The thought of Amanda and James making conversation with my parents fills me with dread and I feel quite sick as a result.

We head to the nearby pizzeria and sit awkwardly at a large round table.

As soon as we order, James looks at my father and says politely, "I understand you were Jack's headmaster. I think I remember you, but I never visited the school that much. It was always Amanda's department."

My heart sinks as I see the look in my father's eye. This was always his pet hate when the fathers didn't show an interest in their child's education.

Amanda nods vigorously, "Yes, I must apologise for my husband, Mr Gray. He was always so busy with work and his... um... hobbies, he never had much time for his family."

The air grows thick with tension, and I notice Jack turn pale under the subdued lighting. Luckily, my mother is a master at getting out of an awkward situation and says brightly, "I know, it's quite normal these days. Work takes up so much of our time, there's never really any time for the things we would much rather be doing. I must say, though, I'm guessing you were so proud of your son because, from what I've heard, he was a brilliant footballer."

James nods and smiles at Jack proudly. "I am proud of my son and not just because he was good at sports. I'm proud of the kind, loving son he turned out to be, despite minimal input on my part."

He gazes across to Amanda and smiles. Reaching out, he takes her hand and says sincerely, "I owe everything to my wife. She has worked so hard bringing up our children and all credit must go to her."

To my surprise, I see tears well in Amanda's eyes and she looks at James as if she's seeing a man she long forgot existed. It's a little awkward watching them because this feels so private, but I can't tear my eyes from the scene in front of me.

James looks at Jack and says, "I know it's not been the easiest of childhoods. I have worked most of it and any family time has been fraught, to say the least. Looking back on it all makes me wonder why I placed so much importance on work when I had everything I wanted already."

The silence in the air is palpable, as nobody wants to be the one to follow that little speech. Then Amanda says softly, "Thank you, James."

I notice his hand is still clasping hers and as I catch Jack's eyes, I see the emotion in them as he smiles happily. The moment is interrupted as the waitress delivers our food and normal service resumes, but it leaves me with the hope that things may change for Jack's parents. I certainly hope so.

Dinner is nowhere near as bad as I expected and as we all make our separate ways home, I think back on an eventful evening. Jack is also quiet and when he drops me off, he says thoughtfully, "You know, tonight was quite the eye opener."

I nod in agreement. "Yes, first there was Soraya, or whatever her name is. I'm pretty sure she's got a few skeletons that need releasing from the closet."

Jack grins. "Regional champions for parents. You kept that quiet."

"You never asked." I grin, and Jack shakes his head. "We don't stand a chance of winning with such stiff competition."

I shake my head. "I doubt they'll even take part. My parents have a lot of obligations. It comes with the territory of what they do. They manage the odd evening out, but to commit to something on a regular basis is a luxury neither of them can afford."

"They still find time for each other, though. Maybe that's where my parents went wrong."

He looks so sad I reach for his hand and squeeze it gently. "Maybe they realised an important lesson tonight. Who knows, it may help rekindle what they had once."

Pulling me close, he whispers, "Promise me we will always have time for each other, Nelly. Don't go hurtling off down a different path and leave me behind. Who knows where our particular journey will end, but it's one I want to take with you and I've never felt like that before?"

As Jack kisses me under the light of a harvest moon, I make a silent vow to us. Whatever this is, I will make sure I work at making it magnificent. If it turns out not to be, then I'll know in my heart that I gave it my best shot. I just hope when the glow wears off, Jack will feel the same.

CHAPTER 31

The next few weeks follow the same pattern. Work, practice and dance classes twice a week. Jack and I have been taking secret lessons from my parents, which was strange at first but not now. I can see why they were champions because, despite appearances, they can certainly move. I'm also enjoying spending lots of time pressed against Jack, perfecting our sexy moves. If anything, it has brought us closer together and I can only hope it has worked the same magic on Amanda and James.

Tonight, however, is the final class before the finalists are announced and everything is riding on it. If I have my way, we will be one of those couples, and not Ken and Violet.

Ken has kept his distance from me, and I have tried to do the same with Violet. We have been unsuccessful in tracing Soraya Bellfield because she isn't on any of the usual social media platforms, and nobody appears to have heard of her. It's all very annoying and so I can only hope Plan A works because Plan B is proving a dead end.

Jack and I head to the Armitage Centre for the last time if we don't make it through.

We are among the first couples to arrive and take up our usual position in the corner.

In total, there must be about ten couples who have headed here religiously every week.

Jack nudges me as his parents arrive and I am pleased to see they appear in a good mood. James is holding Amanda's hand, and she is laughing at something he says. Jack whispers, "They've been a lot more relaxed with each other these past few weeks. Maybe Aunt Alice was right, and all they needed was the excuse to reconnect."

They head our way and I smile as Amanda says in a low voice, "So, here we are, judgement day. If James and I don't go through, we can tell Aunt Alice we gave it our best shot, but it wasn't good enough."

I smile reassuringly. "You'll be fine. You're both really good and much better than most of the other couples here."

James grins. "Well, we have been taking extra lessons."

I stare at them in surprise. "I never knew that."

Amanda laughs softly as Jack says, "When?"

She shakes her head. "That's our secret, and we'll only tell you if we are successful."

We notice Violet and Ken arriving and Amanda pulls a face. "Can that woman sink any lower?"

I stifle a giggle because Violet looks as if she has kitted them both out for an episode of Strictly Come Dancing. She is wearing a sparkling spandex gold dress with multicoloured ruffles that swing around her waist. She has a sequined flower in her hair and her lips are painted bright red with what appears to be shiny lip gloss over them.

Ken is wearing a white tuxedo with a matching red sequined cummerbund, and I feel sorry for him. He's obviously uncomfortable with his hair slicked back with sparkly gel. He looks like one of those older men who is desperate to stay young. They look totally ridiculous and Jack laughs as he whispers, "We don't stand a chance. I mean, look at them. They look the part, so obviously they are the best dancers here."

Giggling, I point to Cilla, who is staring at them as if they are the answer to her prayers. She is gushing over the outfits as she chats animatedly with Violet. I don't miss the triumphant look Violet throws me as Cilla claps her hands and says excitedly, "Attention everybody, we will shortly begin, but I must just congratulate Violet and Ken on stepping up and making such a huge effort with their costumes. It's this degree of professionalism that goes a long way with the judges. It makes them stand out and will probably get them extra points for effort, so well done and as a reward, you can start us off."

Violet glances around smugly, as Ken takes her in his arms. The music begins, and I watch as they begin gyrating to the music. The concentration on their faces is quite comical, and I notice Violet counting under her breath as Ken struggles to keep up.

Jack whispers, "Poor old guy. No prizes for guessing who's really wearing the trousers in that relationship."

James laughs. "Look at his face. I'm sure he would rather be sitting at home watching a crime thriller or football. It's obvious this is a huge ordeal for him."

They all laugh, but I can't join in. Poor Ken. This is the last thing he wants to be doing, and being the focus of so much attention is obviously making him feel uncomfortable. My heart goes out to him, and I wonder if he looks back on those days with Patty more fondly than he left them.

It's soon time for the rest of us to join in and I'm aware that tonight we must pull out all the stops. Jack is serious for once and we give everything we've got to delivering a flawless performance. Some of the couples here aren't interested in progressing through to the competition, which helps, but I'd say at least five couples are doing everything they can to make it.

So, it's with a lot of nerves between us that we stare expectantly at Cilla as she reads out the names of the couples going through to the regional finals.

In true Cilla fashion, she stands in the centre of the room under a lone spotlight.

"Ladies and gentlemen. Now, the moment you have all been waiting for. My announcement of who will progress through to represent us in the regional finals. This hasn't been an easy decision because there are some worthy contenders here, but in no particular order, here is my decision."

She pauses for maximum effect and then squeals, "Violet and Ken."

My heart sinks as Violet pulls a reluctant Ken through the crowd and thrusts their joined hands into the air with a triumphant look at me. You would think she had won the whole competition as she beams around the room and acts as if she's shocked and overawed by the whole occasion. James laughs, "Stupid tart."

Amanda stares at him in horror and then her eyes crinkle and she laughs out loud. "For once I agree with you, James."

Jack shakes his head as Cilla says loudly. "Now, who will be joining them?"

Once again, she pauses for dramatic effect and says, "Sandra and Terry."

My heart sinks when I realise that at least one of us is going to be disappointed, and Jack squeezes my hand. "Don't worry, Nelly. If it doesn't work out, at least we tried."

Suddenly, things get serious, and my heart thumps madly. What if we don't get through?

Once Sandra and Terry have had their moment of triumph, Cilla says with excitement. "And now for the final place. This was a difficult decision, but there can only be one more couple going through. It all came down to the last dance, but I can now confirm that the third couple going through are…. Amanda and James."

Pushing my disappointment aside, I hug Amanda and then James, saying happily, "Congratulations, you deserve it."

They appear to be in shock, and Jack laughs. "Now you've got to work even harder to beat Violet because we're counting on you both."

James shakes his head and then laughing, lifts Amanda off the floor and spins her around as she laughs in shock.

Even though Violet is enjoying her moment of victory as she smirks in my direction, I am so happy for Jack's parents. Jack pulls me against him and whispers, "I'm sorry, babe, I let you down."

I stare at him in astonishment. "Of course you didn't. It was probably me, anyway. I've always had two left feet and certainly never took after either of my parents. No, you haven't let me down, Jack. To be honest, I'm glad it was your parents and not us, anyway."

As we watch Amanda and James lining up next to the other winners, I notice the sparkle in their eyes and the flush on Amanda's cheeks. I have never seen her looking so happy and for a moment she looks relaxed and content. James appears to have shed whatever burden he always appears to carry around with him, and they look happier than I have ever seen them.

I say sincerely, "The right people won, Jack. I'm happy for them. We must make sure they win the competition because now it's more personal than ever."

CHAPTER 32

Two weeks later, I have a visitor and glance up in surprise as a familiar face heads through the door of the shop.

"Aunt Alice!"

She smiles sweetly. "Hello, dear. I hope you don't mind, but I wanted to come and see this delicious emporium for myself."

I wipe my sweaty palms on my jeans and say self-consciously, "Well, here it is. My dream come true."

Aunt Alice stares around her with obvious approval. "I must say, Nelly, this shop is everything I thought it would be. You have done a good job here."

I feel a surge of pride as we look around and smile happily. "I love this place. It's all I ever wanted and if I could change one thing, it's that I have a few more customers."

Aunt Alice says with concern. "I feel a little responsible for that, darling."

"Why, it's not your fault the town is quiet."

She sighs. "No, but I haven't made it easy for you either. When I instructed Jack to open his business, I never really thought about how it would affect the competition."

Shrugging, I offer her a taster chocolate; a smooth dark chocolate that blows your mind. "It's fine. To be honest, Jack's business brings more people in than it keeps away. As he said, he doesn't sell a lot of chocolate and the fact they stare at my window from across the street while they're having a coffee helps me. Most of the time, they head across after they've finished and buy something."

She smiles with relief. "That's good to hear. You know, when I set my challenges, I never expected them to be carried out with such sincerity. My family isn't known for that emotion, and I thought they would just pay lip service to it. They've surprised me, in a good way."

I nod in agreement. "I'm glad. They have really tried their best; I can vouch for that."

Aunt Alice smiles. "I know they have. Anyway, can you take a break and keep an old lady company and join me for a spot of tea and cake?"

I wave around at the empty shop. "I think the rush can wait for half an hour. I'll just pop a sign on the door and tell any customers where I'll be if they need anything."

She smiles as I hang my usual sign and we head across the road together.

As we take our seats at one of the little tables that sit proudly on the pavement outside More Than Chocolate, Aunt Alice sighs. "You know, this was always my dream. How lovely to be able to work doing something you love. Not many of us get that luxury."

I nod in agreement as Emma heads our way and says abruptly, "Morning, Nelly, what can I get you?"

Aunt Alice raises her eyes and says pointedly, "Excuse me, is Jack available?"

Emma shakes her head. "No, he's busy."

"Then please can you interrupt him and tell him that his aunt would like a word?"

Emma sighs. "OK, if you insist, but I was told he didn't want to be disturbed."

She stares at me with a gleam in her eye and says sweetly, "He never does when he's locked in the stock room with an attractive supplier."

As she flounces off, Aunt Alice shakes her head. "My goodness, that's a woman scorned if ever I saw one."

I roll my eyes. "You could say that, though in her defence, they went out once and I don't think she's accepted it's over."

"Hmm. Thank goodness Jack woke up and saw what was really important."

"What, that it's best to settle for someone who has fewer looks, much more personality, and a few brain cells that haven't been damaged under the tanning bench?"

Aunt Alice grins wickedly. "I agree with everything you just said, except for one thing."

"Which one?"

"Fewer looks. If you think looking like a plastic doll from a toyshop is good looking, you are seriously mistaken. That girl had so much makeup holding her face together, I'm surprised she could move her lips to speak. No, girls like that dress to attract other girls, not men. They think it makes them look beautiful, but it just makes them appear uglier. Men want a real woman, not a synthetic excuse for one. If anything, she is a caricature, and I feel sorry for her."

We look up as Jack comes racing outside, smiling broadly. He kisses us in turn and says, "This is an unexpected treat. Have you ordered?"

Aunt Alice nods. "Yes, and I must say, Jack, your staff could do with some more training. That girl was most unpleasant."

Jack smiles apologetically. "I'm sorry about Emma. She can be a little... um... emotional, but overall, she works well enough."

Aunt Alice gestures to the seat beside her. "Take a seat, Jack, because I have something I need to say."

I don't miss the anxious expression in Jack's eyes as he does what he's told, and we peer at Aunt Alice expectantly.

She smiles and says in a low voice. "I've come to say goodbye."

I'm a little anxious as I try to guess the meaning behind the sentence. Goodbye as in going away, or goodbye as in she really is leaving – life!

Ever since I heard about her will, I haven't been convinced it's as straight forward as everyone thinks.

Jack says with surprise. "What do you mean, goodbye?"

She laughs. "I'm heading back to Miami. To be honest, I would have gone weeks ago, but I was intrigued by how things would progress with your challenges. However, the pull of the sun is too great, and I need to recharge my sunshine batteries. The house is depressing me, and I have grown tired of all my friends."

She says in a whisper, "They're nice enough, but so old, if you know what I mean. Always moaning about their illnesses and aches and pains. It's enough to sink me into a depression."

She laughs out loud. "No, it's time to head overseas and enjoy life again. However, I didn't want to leave before I wrapped things up here first because I won't be back for several months if I can help it."

I feel in the way and say nervously, "Um… do you want me to give you some privacy?"

She reaches out and grasps my hand, saying firmly, "Absolutely not. You're one of the family now, Nelly, and can stay to hear what I have to say."

She stares across at Jack and her eyes soften. "My gorgeous great-nephew. How I love spending time with you and of everyone, I think I'm proud of you the most. You have turned into a fine young man and make me the proudest great aunt in history."

She looks across at me and smiles. "Nelly is a super girl and I'm glad you saw beyond the obvious and reached for the stars, because Nelly is a rare thing. She has a heart, and that is why I think you will be happy together. There is a depth to her that doesn't come with everyone and so make sure you treat her right and learn from your parent's mistakes."

I feel a little uncomfortable as Jack nods slowly. He glances across at me and smiles sweetly, saying gruffly, "I am lucky, Aunt Alice. I realise that."

Shifting in my seat, I hope they change this topic of conversation because this is embarrassing. Luckily, she turns to him and says seriously, "I have decided to give you your inheritance, Jack. You have done everything I asked of you and did it well. This place is thriving, and it's all because of you. You have put your heart and soul into realising what was my dream, and I can't thank you enough. However, I don't expect you to chain yourself to it forever. Take the money and do with it what you want. Employ a manager, close the shop, or do whatever you want because life's too short to do something you don't want to. Go and travel and see the world because it's a big place to enjoy. All I ask is that you stay true to yourself and approach everything with caution and care. Don't act on a whim and think everything through, because success needs good planning."

Jack stares at her in shock and she smiles sadly. "I know things haven't been easy at home for years. Your parents are good people and I hoped their challenge would bring them closer. I think it has to a degree, but I'm wondering if it will be enough."

Jack stares at her morosely and she reaches out and takes his hand in hers. "Whatever happens, they are your parents. They love you and have always wanted to do the right thing for both you and Ariadne. If the right thing is to go their separate ways, you must respect their decision. There is no certainty that what seems right at the time will last forever. Real life has a habit of getting in the way and sometimes it's for the best. If your parents can't re-discover what made them love each other in the first place, then they should be allowed to find it elsewhere. They owe it to themselves to live the best lives they can and that may be apart. It won't change what they think of you, and you will be happier if they are happy."

Jack says sadly, "Do you think they will split up?"

She shrugs. "I think they will, but I hope they won't. I am going to give them the inheritance and, if anything, it will give them the choice. Your mother's company will continue. Your father can still run it, even if he lives elsewhere. Your mother would be happy to let him because she was never interested in it in the first place. She was chained to something she never wanted, and it dragged her under. Maybe if they break those chains, they will fly. Be happy for them, whatever they choose, because they deserve to live the best lives they can."

She smiles and says softly. "The same goes for your sister. I may never understand what goes on in that young lady's mind, but I'm proud of the woman she is becoming. To be honest, I thought she would fold first and was waiting to see how quickly that would happen. Of everyone, she has surprised me the most. She has embraced her challenge like a true hero. I visited the home she works at and saw the genuine love she has for the residents, and they have for her. She has taken an impossible situation and made it her own. Ariadne has qualities that are genuine, wrapped in a gaudy packaging. She can't change the decade she was born into, and I have to accept this is their world now. I may not understand it, but times are changing fast. Things I once considered important still are, but in a different way. Technology has moved on and there are many more opportunities out there for the young. Ariadne sees those opportunities and is right to pursue them. I am disappointed in my own lack of foresight in judging her by my own standards. So, Ariadne gets her inheritance and if she wants to blow the lot on a holiday, I'm not going to judge her for it. However, I think of everyone, she will surprise me the most."

She smiles and then turns to me and says warmly. "You're a good girl, Nelly. You remind me of myself and what's not to love about that?"

She laughs and we smile as she claps her hand with excitement. "So, I am going to love you and leave you and look forward to seeing what the next chapter holds for you all. Will Jack and Nelly throw everything in and travel the world? Will Ariadne become a superstar on social media and live life jetting all over the world, or will she train to be a nurse instead? And what about your parents, Jack? Will they celebrate their golden wedding anniversary one day and look back on a life well spent, or will they meet new partners and discover things about themselves they never knew? That's what's so amazing about life. We never know where it's going to take us, but we can't get hung up on the details. Just enjoy the ride and make sure any decisions you make are the best ones for you because when the dust claims our bodies and our souls are set free, we ultimately leave on our own."

She stands and places an envelope on the table in front of Jack and a lump forms in my throat as I see the tears in her eyes. Pulling him towards her, she says softly, "I love you, Jack. Make sure you live the best life you can."

The tears fall as I see Jack hug his aunt tightly and say gruffly, "Thank you, Aunt Alice. I mean that with everything in my heart. I love you and make sure we see you soon."

Wiping her eyes, she sniffs and turns to me. "Come here, Nelly. I haven't forgotten you either."

I stare at her in disbelief as she hands me another envelope. She laughs at the shock on my face as she says softly, "This is for you. I felt bad that I caused you problems with your business in encouraging Jack to open opposite. This covers the rent for a year and, like Jack, I want you to use the money wisely. Don't feel as if you must use it to keep the business going if there's something you would rather be doing. Remember to sample every sweet delight in the chocolate box of life and look back on a life well spent. I should know because I'm still doing it. Don't do what's expected, do what's right and sometimes the hardest part is recognising what that is."

As I hug her tightly, the tears spill onto her shoulder as I say gruffly, "Thank you so much. I can't possibly accept this, it's too much."

She pulls back and says sharply, "Nonsense. It's nothing, really. One thing I have is money. Lots and lots of money and I want to see it do some good while I'm still alive. I have more than I need, so I want to make someone else's life a little easier. Just write and visit me from time to time and tell me of all the amazing things you are doing."

She whispers, "I hope it works out with Jack, but I'm not holding you to it. He will have to sharpen up – a lot if he wants to hold on to you."

She winks, and I laugh as Jack takes my hand and smiles. "I'll look after her and we will definitely be out to visit you in Miami as soon as we can."

Smiling, Aunt Alice places some money on the table and winks. "For the tea and cakes. Now, make me proud. Well, I must be off. I haven't time to stand gossiping, I have a flight to catch – I'm going home."

As we say our goodbyes, again - I can't quite believe what just happened. In fact, I'm in shock for days because lately the unexpected has become normality. However, now I need the magic to work for a little longer because next week it's the salsa competition finals.

CHAPTER 33

Fair Meadow Halls. The name is spelt out in lights as we stand in line outside. Tonight is the final of the salsa competition and the winner will walk off twenty thousand pounds richer.

I'm nervous for Amanda and Jack, but if they don't win, it will be fine, just as long as Violet and Ken don't.

I haven't seen much of them and made sure to leave three months' rent up front under their door to keep Violet away from me. I felt guilty using Aunt Alice's money, but Jack assured me it was what she intended it for anyway and not to worry.

Jack and I have grown closer since she left and spend every minute together that we can. I feel a little guilty that I have neglected my friends, so have asked them along tonight to join us.

As I glance behind me, I notice Richie standing beside Roger, looking excited and he says loudly, "Ooh, I can't wait to see the men dressed in their lycra and sequins. You know this is pure genius. We should take it up, Roger."

Roger rolls his eyes. "I may have a new knee, but it doesn't work miracles. I'm facing months of physio before my dancing days are back again and…"

"Oh, give it a rest. You know, next time you have surgery, remind me to book a world cruise for one - for a year. You've become really boring, you know."

I grin as they continue bickering, but I know it's all part of their act. Richie and Roger are like an old married couple that enjoy winding each other up. They are always laughing and love each other with the fiercest kind of love possible.

I grin as my eyes fall to my friend Angela, who is standing hand in hand with Gary, the chocolate rep who I introduced to her. They have been secretly dating ever since and I was happy when they told me. They make such a cute couple and I've never seen Angela so happy. She smiles as she sees me looking and says with excitement. "I wish you were in the final. You must have been cheated."

Jack laughs. "Spoken like a true friend. No, the right decision was made. Nelly and I are best left dancing privately."

I blush as they all laugh and then the line starts moving and Richie yells, "OMG, this is it! I can't wait to letch at all those gyrating bodies. Come on. We should try to get a seat in the front row."

We join the crowd milling towards the ticket lines and soon find ourselves seated in the second row in the middle of the large theatre. As we wait, I whisper to Jack, "Are your parents nervous?"

He nods. "I think so. Luckily, they've been kept busy so haven't had much time to dwell on it."

He peers around and says with interest, "Are your parents here yet?"

Checking my phone, I note the text my mum sent earlier. "They're helping your parents with some last-minute preparations. They'll probably take their seats just before it starts."

As we wait, I laugh when I think about my parents and

Jack's. They have grown quite close, as the extra lessons James and Amanda took were with them. Despite what I first thought, they get on well and are now good friends. I really believe James and Amanda are trying to make a go of things because they are spending a lot more time together and appear to be getting along well.

Suddenly, Jack gets a text, and he looks up with excitement. "Show time."

An anxious smile breaks out across my face, as I say nervously, "What, now?"

He nods and takes my hand purposefully.

"Come on, we need to see this."

Ignoring the curious stares of my friends, I follow Jack backstage. My heart is pounding, and I say nervously, "What if it doesn't work?"

He shrugs. "As Aunt Alice said, you can but try. Some things aren't meant to be, and we can't help that."

As I follow Jack, I see Ariadne gesturing madly from a doorway. "Hurry up, guys, they're almost here. You don't want to miss this."

We enter a room where all the contestants are getting ready. It's full to the brim with sequinned costumes, little tables with mirrors attached, that are covered in trays of make-up and hair extensions.

I spy Amanda and James laughing at something my mother says and they smile as we draw near.

I hug my parents and then say fearfully, "I hope this works."

Amanda nods. "It will. Trust me."

Glancing around, I spot Violet and Ken getting ready nearby and as she sees me, Violet sneers. I take a moment to throw her my most withering look before I'm aware of Ken's expression changing quite drastically. He appears stunned and as I turn around, I can why.

Heading into the room is a spectacle that leaves me breathless. Looking utterly amazing and like something out of a fairy story, is Patty. She is dressed like a princess and has been totally transformed. She's wearing a silver figure-hugging gown that clings to her curves in all the right places. Her hair is styled and piled on top of her head and woven with silver jewels that sparkle in the spotlights. She looks ten years younger as her make-up accentuates a beauty that never really dulled. Patty looks magical and I say to Ariadne, "Oh, well done. You are amazing."

With obvious pride in her voice, Ariadne says sincerely, "It was easy. True beauty shines from within. I just helped it out."

I glance behind me and register Ken's astonishment. He can't take his eyes off Patty, and I note every emotion passing across his face. Then I see Violet's expression and dance a victory parade inside my head. "Got ya!"

Her expression is one of pure, unadulterated lust. The pound signs have revealed themselves in her eyes because she is looking at only one thing.

Accompanying Patty is a man who is every inch the rich playboy he portrays. Godfrey has scrubbed up like we knew he would and is playing his part perfectly. He is dressed in a tight-fitting dark suit, with a silver tie and polished black shoes. His hair is gelled back, and he gazes around him with the air of the super-rich as he looks down his nose at everyone before him. His well-educated voice floats across the room, as he says loudly, "Darling, let me find you a seat. You must rest before the competition. As soon as we win, I'll treat you to the villa in the Caribbean as a thank you."

Violet can't stare at him hard enough and I watch as she moves away from Ken and heads towards the glamorous couple. However, Ken moves faster and reaches Patty first and says with emotion, "Oh my god, Patty. Is that really you?"

We shamefully listen in as Patty nods coolly. "Hello, Ken. It's been a while."

WHEN CUPID MISSED

Violet stares at them and says in disbelief, "Is this... her?"

Ken ignores her and says softly, "You look beautiful, Patty."

She shrugs. "Thank you. Anyway, I should introduce my partner, Godfrey Rosenbalm. You may have heard of his family; they own the steel company, Rosenbalm Industries."

Violet thrusts out her hand and takes hold of Godfrey's, squeezing it and giggling, "Charmed. My name's Violet. Maybe we could swap notes on dancing. I'm quite the professional."

Godfrey looks at her with distaste. "I'm sorry. What did you say your name was?"

She bats her eyelashes and says in a girly voice, "Violet Monroe. You may have heard of me because I am quite famous in my own way."

Godfrey frowns. "Yes, I thought that's what you said. It's funny, but I could have sworn somebody told me you were Soraya Bellfield."

Violet visibly pales and says quickly, "No, you're mistaken. My name's Violet. You must be mistaking me for somebody else."

Reaching inside his pocket, Godfrey pulls out his phone and taps into it. Then he holds it up and says loudly, "No, I don't think so."

Ken looks at the phone sharply and then takes it from Godfrey, saying incredulously, "I don't believe it."

Ariadne marches over and says with disgust. "Godfrey is right. Soraya Bellfield is a known con artist. She cheated a man called Max Williams out of a small fortune before fleeing the country. They never found her, but then she popped up again, this time as Simone Hughes."

She holds up the phone with yet another picture of Violet and reads, "Simone Hughes was questioned by police amid fraud allegations, when she cheated her fiancé William Edwards out of a small fortune. Nothing could be proven, and she was last seen leaving the county protesting her innocence."

Ariadne sneers. "So, it appears you make a career out meeting gullible men and cheating them out of their money. You call yourself a different name every time and even though you operate within the law, you break every moral one. The men believe you love them and want to make a future with them. You take whatever you can and then leave for the next best thing. It's just a shame you picked the wrong man this time because I happen to be rather a good professional stalker. There is nothing I can't find out on social media and you, my dear, have just been found out. What do you have to say for yourself?"

Violet stares around her in amazement and shrivels under the hostile looks directed her way.

Ken says incredulously, "Is this true, Violet? Tell me she's lying."

My father steps forward and says firmly, "She's not lying, Ken. I recognised Soraya as soon as I saw her. She was excluded from school years ago when she accused a colleague of mine of sexual indiscretions. She blackmailed him, saying she was going to ruin his career unless he paid her a vast sum of money. He was married at the time with a family and the scandal ruined him. Soraya was expelled and moved to another part of the country. I can see she never learned from the experience. If anything, she only learned how to succeed the next time."

Violet yells, "So what? I do nothing wrong. I give gullible fools a reason to enjoy life." She waves at Ken. "As if I would ever be attracted to an old man like this."

She throws Ken a disgusted look and says angrily, "I give them something to look forward to in life, and they give me their money. I wouldn't be interested if it wasn't for that. No, I haven't done anything wrong, so call the police if you want to, but you will all look as stupid as you are."

She turns to Ken and sneers. "Look at you. You're a joke. As if a woman like me would ever really love a man like you."

Suddenly, her head flies back and we hear a loud crack as a hand connects with her cheek. We stare in shock as Patty stands in front of Violet, fuming with rage.

She says angrily, "How dare you? Ken is worth a million of you. You're scum of the worst kind and deserve to rot in prison for crimes against humanity. How dare you treat a good, honest man this way and wreck other people's lives for your own gain? Shame on you, you despicable woman and if I ever see you again, you had better start running because I think nothing of shooting vermin on my farm and I class you as the worst kind."

Violet holds her hand to her cheek and stares at Patty in disbelief. Then she looks around at the hostile faces that surround her and sneers, "I'm going because why would I want to spend another minute with losers like you?"

She turns and sneers at Ken. "Stupid old fool. Men like you will never learn."

She heads off through the crowd, leaving everyone staring after her in shock. I look at Ken and go to comfort him, but Patty gets there first.

Taking his hand, she says softly, "I think you need a new partner, Ken."

He gazes at her with a soft look which brings tears to my eyes and says with emotion. "No, Patty. I should never have let go of the old one."

Suddenly, we hear, "Places, places, everyone. The competition is about to begin."

Cilla races over and stares around with surprise. "Where's Violet? Is she taking a natural break?"

Ken laughs bitterly. "Something like that. No, she was just standing in for my real partner, Cilla. This is Patty, and she is a million times better than Violet."

Cilla looks surprised but merely shrugs and says loudly, "OK, places everyone, places."

As the room begins to thin out, I watch Jack hug Amanda and Ariadne and James join in. They all look so happy, and I hope with all my heart, things work out for them.

As I stand back, Godfrey says softly, "You know, I could quite see myself as an actor. That was fun. Maybe I should pursue it as a career."

I say with interest. "What do you do for a living, Godfrey?"

He shrugs. "I'm training to be a surgeon."

As he heads off to find Ariadne, I pick my jaw up from the floor. God help us all.

CHAPTER 34

"Hurry up Jack, we'll miss our flight."

"It's ok, we've got ages. Stop worrying."

I stare around in disbelief at all the bags we're taking and shake my head. "Hardly the backpacking dream, is it?"

He laughs. "Blame Ariadne for that. She wouldn't know the meaning of the term - travelling light."

He slips his arm around my waist and pulls me close, whispering, "I love you, Nelly."

I say softly, "I love you right back."

"Put her down, Jack. There's plenty of time for all that when we're there."

Reluctantly, Jack pulls away and Ariadne casts a critical eye over the bags. "Have we all got luggage labels? I will freak out if any one of my bags goes missing. I need absolutely everything in them because I intend to take lots of great Instagram photos and require every single outfit."

Jack groans as he tries to lift one of her cases. "There is such a thing as a weight restriction, you know. I'll be amazed if this one passes the test."

Rolling her eyes, Ariadne replies, "Godfrey never takes

much, so I've used his allowance as well. We've also been upgraded so you get more allowance. It's the best economical solution all round and just think of the shots I'll get reclining in first class."

Jack shakes his head as Amanda rushes in. "Who hasn't given daddy their passports? You know how he likes to be in charge of the paperwork."

Ariadne shouts, "Oh, for goodness' sake, for the last time, I gave it to him yesterday along with Godfrey's."

Amanda nods. "I told him that, but he's panicking as usual. It's probably best if you get Jack and Godfrey to sneak a few bags in the taxi before he sees them. You know he'll blow a fuse when he sees the stuff you're taking."

Jack grins. "He can talk. His case is the biggest one of all."

Amanda laughs. "Although it is half full. I know, distract him, Jack and Ariadne and I will fill it with the toiletries. That should even out the weight issue and he'll never know if I get to it first at the other end."

I shake my head as they set about their task and Jack rolls his eyes. "They're all mad."

I gaze at him anxiously. "What about Angela? Do you think she'll be ok?"

"More than ok and it's not as if she hasn't got help."

I congratulate myself that Angela agreed to look after the shop for me. She was pleased to leave her job and, along with Gary, they promised to keep Chocolatti running while we're away. Once again, I feel the nerves surfacing and say, "Are we doing the right thing, Jack? What if it all goes badly wrong?"

He pulls me close and says softly, "We aren't. We're doing what we always dreamed of and have planned everything down to the last detail."

I smile and try to relax. "You're right. I'm just being silly."

James yells from downstairs. "The taxis here. Bring those cases down before I lose the will to live."

Grumbling, Jack picks the nearest one up and struggles to transport it downstairs. I laugh as I hear James swearing as he takes it from him, yelling, "What the hell is in here, the bricks from the house? There is a bloody weight restriction, you know. Whose is this?"

I laugh as I hear Jack say with amusement. "I think it's yours, actually."

The air turns blue as James lets rip and Godfrey rolls his eyes. "They're all mad."

I nod and watch him pluck one of the smaller bags from the pile and move towards the door and I say with interest, "When do you start your placement, Godfrey?"

He pulls a face. "One month from today. Then the work really starts."

"What you're doing is amazing. You will save lives and make things count. I really admire you."

He shrugs. "Possibly. I hope I don't mess up though. It's quite a responsibility."

I smile reassuringly. "You'll be great. You know, I misjudged you when I first met you. I suppose I never took the time to get to know you before making up my mind."

He shrugs. "We all do it, Nelly. Isn't that human nature? We see a stereotype and believe in that. Take Ariadne, for instance. She gets misjudged every day of her life yet never lets it bother her. It's why I love her so much. She doesn't care what people think and does what she wants, anyway. I'm not sure why we're expected to look or act a certain way if you do a certain job or live a particular lifestyle. I suppose the most interesting people I have met have been the ones that surprised me the most."

He heads off to join the others and I think about what he said. I think we're all guilty of being judgemental. It starts early and never really leaves us. I was judged by who my parents were and the way I dressed, and I judged everyone around me in the same way. It's only when you take time to look behind the facade that you see the true person inside.

I think about Ken and Patty and smile. Ken's head was turned by someone he thought was better, but he soon found out what he had was right all the time. Luckily for them, after a lot of discussion, it all worked out and now they've moved in together and made a commitment to share their lives and everything that involves. I suppose Violet did them a favour in the long run, although it didn't seem that way at the time. I'm not sure what happened to her, and I don't want to know. No doubt she set up some other gullible man and is currently plotting and scheming her way through life. I feel sorry for her because she will never know how amazing life can be when you find that special someone to share it with.

"Nelly, are you ready?"

"Coming."

I grab my bags and head outside. As usual, the family is arguing, which makes me smile.

"Honestly, dad, I told you I needed the extra baggage allowance. You know, I can't wait until we're on that plane and I can put on my noise reduction headphones."

"Amanda, have you set the timer on the boiler? I don't want to be heating fresh air for the next fortnight. Just think about the bill."

"For goodness' sake, James, do I have to think of everything? Of course, I set the timer, but did you remember to renew the travel insurance like I told you?"

"Of course, I did. What do you take me for?"

"Just checking. Now, does anyone need the toilet before we go? Godfrey?"

"Oh, maybe that would be a good idea."

Amanda rolls her eyes as Godfrey flies back into the house and Ariadne shouts, "I'll just check I unplugged my portable charger. I think I left it in the kitchen."

James starts pacing angrily and Jack rolls his eyes. Amanda snaps, "Jack, if I have to tell you one more time about that irritable eye roll, I'll leave you behind."

He says incredulously, "Irritable eye roll now. Can't I do anything right?"

"Just get in the car, Jack."

Amanda looks at me and shakes her head. "I'm sorry, Nelly, you must be tearing your hair out. I'm guessing your family is much more organised when they go on trips."

Laughing, I shake my head. "Not really. I think they're much the same as yours."

Just for a minute, we share a look. Yes, this isn't so unusual, really. It's what being part of a family is all about, and I wouldn't change a thing.

As Godfrey and Ariadne come rushing out, James sighs heavily and Amanda frowns. "James, stop..."

"OK, I get it. No sighing, no swearing, no shouting, no breathing, no laughing, no moaning and no bloody conversation, because whatever I do or say is always bloody wrong."

The taxi driver quickly gets into the car and Amanda looks at James and laughs softly. "I'm sorry, darling. Come on, let's lock up and get on our way. At least you'll be spared the usual driving lecture."

James laughs and reaches for his wife, pulling her close and kisses her so sweetly I think we all breathe a collective sigh. Then he says, "I love you, Amanda. Never forget that."

She strokes the side of his face and says sweetly, "I never did."

CHAPTER 35

"Welcome to Miami!"

Aunt Alice beams at us from the doorway of what promises to be the most luxurious place I have ever stayed in.

She doesn't seem to register that her visitors look tired, dishevelled and on their last nerve, as we all stumble over the threshold of the villa she arranged to be our holiday home for the next two weeks.

Amanda smiles wearily and hugs her aunt. "It's lovely to see you, auntie. That was quite some flight."

Aunt Alice nods. "Yes, it is rather tiresome, but you're here now and can relax knowing you have nothing to do but rest for the next two weeks."

One by one we greet her, and she smiles as she gives me a warm hug when it's my turn. "Nelly, I'm so happy you could make it. How is that lovely little business of yours?"

"It's ticking along nicely, thank you."

She shakes her head. "That was a terrible business with your landlord. I can't wait to hear all the juicy details."

She glances around and smiles warmly. "But not now. You

all need to settle in and sleep off that jet lag. I'll be back first thing tomorrow and fill you in on things here."

As we all make ourselves at home in, I pinch myself that this really happening. This villa is impressive in every way. Marble floors lead off to rooms that would fit my entire apartment in them. Each one of them has its own bathroom and double doors leading out onto a huge patio where an impressive pool takes pride of place.

Jack jumps on the bed with excitement and stretches out, saying happily, "This beats working."

Jumping next to him, I say with contentment, "It sure does. I can't believe we're here, can you?"

Turning to face me, he says softly, "I'm happy, though. I mean, we've got it all now, haven't we? Our businesses are doing well, and we are able to leave them in capable hands while we go off travelling. I have the most amazing girlfriend who I never thought I'd find, and my parents seem happier than they have in years. It's funny how things work out."

I reach up and push a lock of hair from his eyes. "I agree. I never thought I'd ever be this happy and that my girl crush would become a reality."

He raises his eyes, "Girl crush?"

Giggling, I sit cross-legged and confess. "You were always my secret crush at school. I imagined us like this many times and lived every fantastic moment of it in my dreams. I had your name written in my notebook surrounded by hearts, and I used to practise signing my name as Nelly Mason."

He looks shocked and I smile reassuringly, "Don't worry, I'm not expecting you to propose or anything, but it's funny how things work out, isn't it? I'm guessing you wouldn't have been happy if someone told you I'd be here now all those years ago. I'm guessing I was the last girl you would ever choose."

Jack sits beside me and pulls my head onto his shoulder, rubbing my back as he says, "I was always fascinated by you,

Nelly. You sat with your head down and would never look anyone in the eye. You had this habit of chewing on your pencil when you were concentrating, and you used to doodle all through maths. You were always the second person to answer a question in class, never the first. When people were asked to choose their teams, you would hide in the background because you were always chosen last. You tried not to let anyone see it bothered you, but I saw the light die in your eyes every time. You carried a green backpack with a blue zip that your mother probably sewed in for you and those brown shoes you wore had black laces, which always struck me as odd. Your favourite class was English because that was when you seemed most animated and the only time I ever saw you really smile."

Tilting my face to his, Jack says with a catch to his voice, "You always fascinated me, Nelly, and I never knew why. Now I do because you were always my girl, even all those years ago. I just never knew it at the time. I'm guessing this was always meant to be, and back then Cupid had a bad day at the office and his arrow missed. That day I asked you to be my girlfriend I meant every word because I should have asked you years ago. Ken wasn't the only one who nearly passed happiness by. But I don't want to think about that because if one good thing came out of Aunt Alice's will, it is you, Nelly. Aunt Alice willed me you, and no amount of money in the world can top that."

Suddenly, words are no longer necessary because actions are all the sweeter. Jack and Nelly, Nelly and Jack, it was written in that childhood notebook and was always meant to be.

EPILOGUE

This is our last night. As we all sit around the fire pit by this amazing pool, I feel the tears building behind my eyes. I can't believe such a magical holiday is over already.

James hands everyone a glass of champagne and then takes his seat beside Amanda and drapes his arm around her shoulders, pulling her close. She smiles up at him and the firelight casts a warm glow across her face as she says, "Thank you, James."

Aunt Alice catches my eye and smiles. It appears that nobody is happier than her to see how well things worked out for them in the end.

She looks around the circle and says happily, "Thanks for coming to visit me. It's been the best two weeks I can ever remember spending with you, and we should all take a minute to reflect on how far we've come since I set my challenges.

Amanda nods. "Well, I must admit, I thought you were mad. I couldn't understand why you thought James and I could use dancing lessons, but I can tell it was just an excuse to get us to spend some time together."

James nods. "You saw what we hadn't seen in a long time.

We grew apart and never made time for each other. The mundane became normality and there was always something, or someone, more important than us."

He smiles with sincerity at Aunt Alice and says softly, "Thank you. It was never about the money with us. We have enough of that to live a good life. The money was nothing compared to the happiness we have reclaimed, and I have fallen in love with my wife all over again. Now the children are settled, we are looking forward to spending more quality time together and putting ourselves first for once."

Aunt Alice appears thoughtful. "Talking about money, did you mind missing out on the prize fund from the competition? That would have been a nice bonus."

Amanda laughs. "As James said, it was never about the money. To be honest, none of us really stood a chance. I mean, where did that couple come from? I'm sure they were professional."

James laughs. "Probably. Couples like that follow the competitions around and clean up. Good luck to them. It was only ever about beating Violet, anyway."

We all laugh as Aunt Alice says, "Whatever happened to Violet, Soraya, or whatever her name was?"

I interrupt. "Nobody knows. She was never seen again, which was a good thing, really. I'm sure wherever she is, she hasn't learned her lesson and is already on to her next victim."

Ariadne giggles. "You know, I really enjoyed cyberstalking her. I felt like a private investigator when I confronted her. I must say, when I stop enjoying life at Sunny Days, I may set up my own private investigation company. It will be such fun."

Godfrey rolls his eyes. "You'd be good at that possum. To be honest, you are good at everything you do. I'm almost certain you would make a better surgeon than me if you put your mind to it."

Ariadne studies her fingernails and shakes her head. "Yuk, I couldn't think of anything worse. These nails are not meant for rummaging around inside the human body. No, I haven't decided what I'm going to do yet, but the money I inherited from you, Aunt Alice, has been put away until I figure it out."

Aunt Alice nods. "Good idea, although I thought you were going on holiday."

"I'm on one now. No, when Godfrey starts working for a living, I'll consider what's next for me. I will probably have to follow his career at first until he's established. I'm happy for now with my Instagram modelling and helping my clients in Sunny Days."

Jack laughs, "Clients?"

She grins. "Yes, they pay me to do their nails, make-up, and hair. I also act as a personal shopper for those who can't get out and my coffee mornings are becoming the stuff of legends. To be honest, Jack, you should hear the stories they tell. Life was certainly more interesting before reality TV. Can you believe they only had three channels to watch and none of them in colour? To be honest, they made their own entertainment, and their stories would make your eyes water."

Jack grins as Aunt Alice turns her attention to us. "What about you? How have things changed?"

Jack takes my hand and smiles gently. "Nelly and I are taking a year out to go travelling. When you all head home tomorrow, we start the next phase of our journey in Mexico. Luckily, Emma and Angela have stepped up to run things in our absence and we intend on making the most of our gap year and seeing as much of the world as possible, thanks to you."

I nod. "Yes, thank you. Without your money, we couldn't have done this, and we want you to know we appreciate everything you've done for us."

Aunt Alice shakes her head. "It was nothing. It gives me pleasure to see my money being put to good use and certainly for travel. I've spent my entire life travelling and the things I have seen make every minute of it well spent."

Amanda turns to her and says, "What about you, Auntie? What's next for you?"

Leaning back, Aunt Alice sighs with contentment, then she laughs softly. "You know, those challenges I set you got me thinking. I took a long look at my own life and where I thought I could improve. Then it hit me hard. There was one dream I never got to realise. One thing I will regret on my deathbed and one thing that will make my life complete."

Her eyes sparkle and she says with excitement. "I'm going to open my own little shop, right here in Miami. A quintessential English tearoom with gifts and chocolates. It's in the early planning stages, but I hope to be open within the next three months. Next time you visit, it will be my turn to show you what I can do."

As the fire flickers in the pit and the stars twinkle in the sky, everything falls into place. Destiny sometimes needs a helping hand and a lot of luck along the way, but all that matters is that you get there in the end.

If you liked this book, you may want to check out

Aunt Daisy's Letter

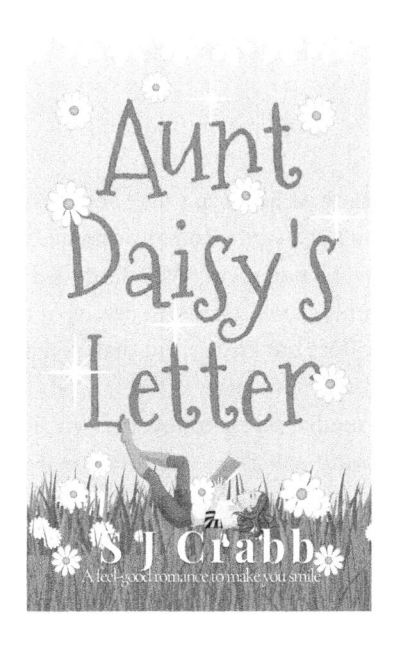

Thank you for reading When Cupid Missed.
If you liked it, I would love if you could leave me a review as I must do all my own advertising.
This is the best way to encourage new readers and I appreciate every review I can get. Please also recommend it to your friends as word of mouth is the best form of advertising. It won't take longer than two minutes of your time, as you only need write one sentence if you want to.
Please note this book is written in UK English which can differ from the US version.

Have you checked out my website? Subscribe to keep updated with any offers or new releases.

sjcrabb.com

Find me on Facebook

Find me on Instagram

Find me on Bookbub

When you visit my website, you may be surprised because I don't just write Romantic comedy.
I also write under the pen names M J Hardy & Harper Adams. I send out a monthly newsletter with details of all my releases and any special offers but aside from that, you don't hear from me very often.
If you like social media, please follow me on mine where I am a lot more active and will always answer you if you reach out to me.
Why not take a look and see for yourself and read Lily's Lockdown, a little scene I wrote to remember the madness when the world stopped and took a deep breath?

Lily's Lockdown

MORE BOOKS BY S J CRABB

More books by S J Crabb

The Diary of Madison Brown
My Perfect Life at Cornish Cottage
My Christmas Boyfriend
Jetsetters
More from Life
A Special Kind of Advent
Fooling in love
Will You
Holly Island
Aunt Daisy's Letter
The Wedding at the Castle of Dreams
My Christmas Romance
Escape to Happy Ever After
Cruising in Love
Coming Home to Dream Valley
Christmas in Dream Valley
New Beginnings in Dream Valley

sjcrabb.com

Printed in Great Britain
by Amazon